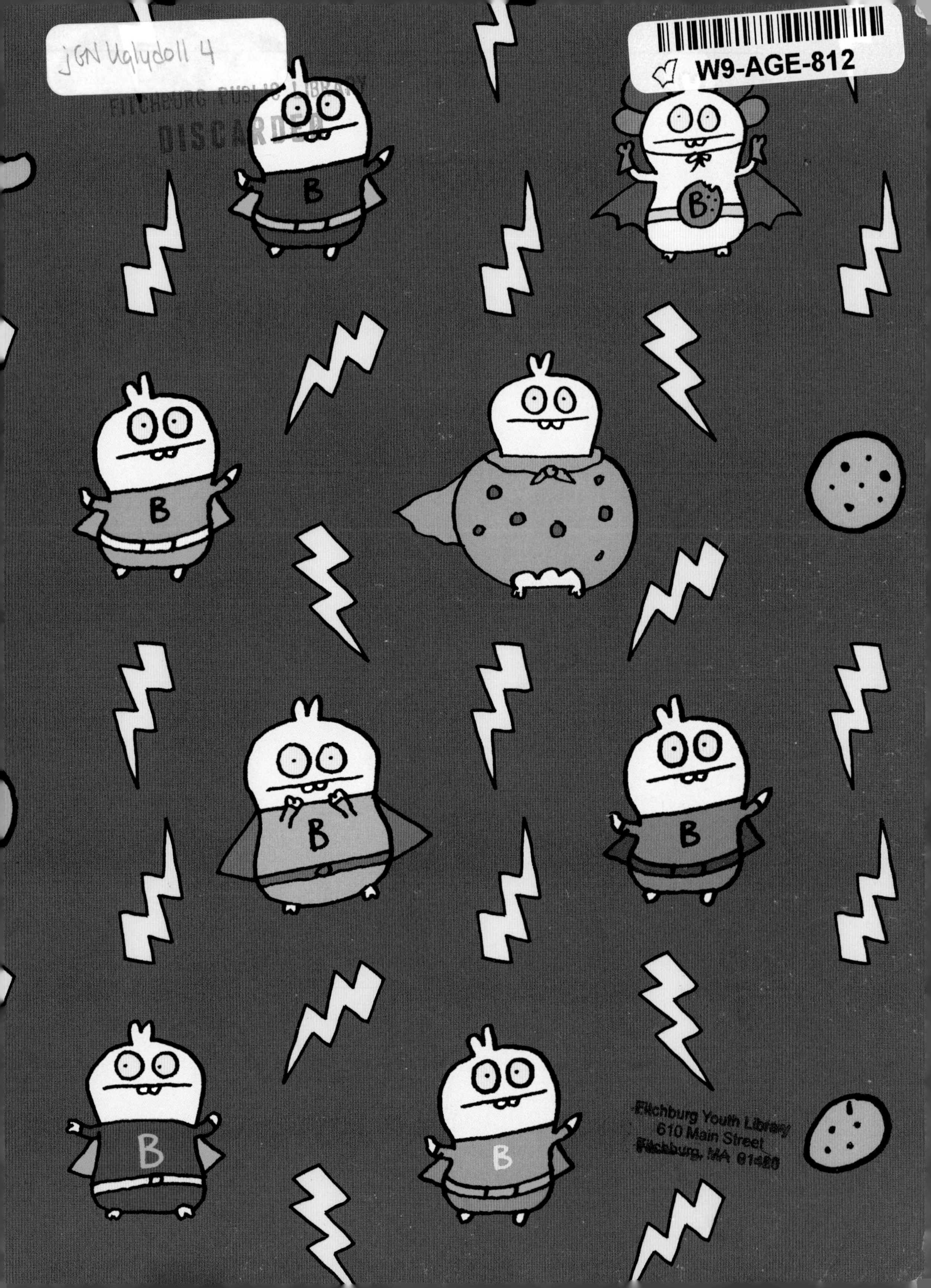

AN UGLYDOLL™ COMIC

MY HERO?

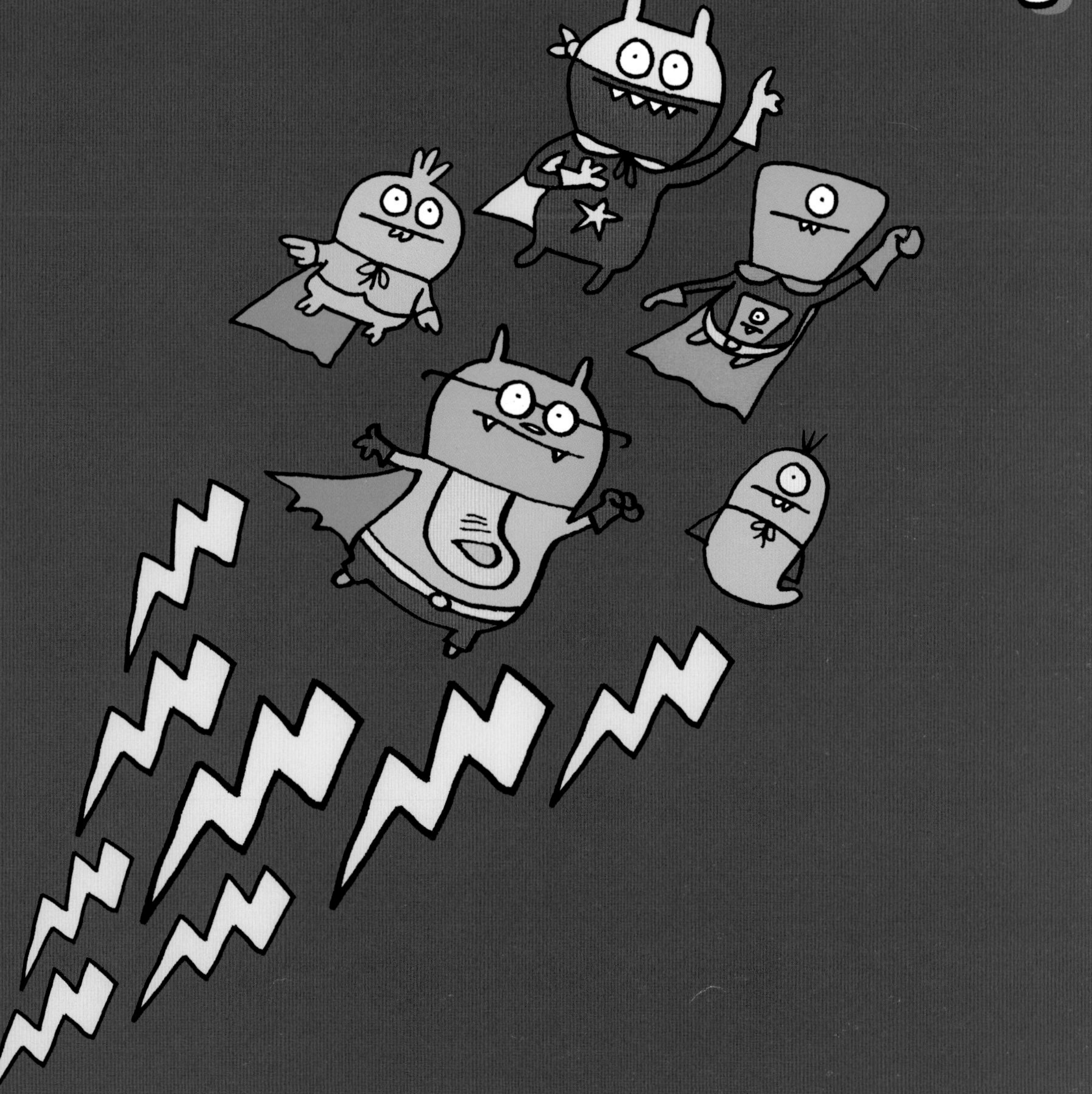

KIM | HORVATH | NICHOLS | JACOBSON | MCGINTY | DVRB | ELLSWORTH | MAD BARBARIANS | MIZUNO

MY HERO?
AN UGLYDOLL COMIC

COVER ART: SUN-MIN KIM AND DAVID HORVATH
COVER AND BOOK DESIGN: FAWN LAU
EDITOR: TRACI N. TODD

Printed in China

Published by VIZ Media, LLC
P.O. Box 77010
San Francisco, CA 94107

10 9 8 7 6 5 4 3 2 1
First printing, April 2014

RATED A FOR ALL AGES
PARENTAL ADVISORY
UGLYDOLL: MY HERO?
is rated A and is suitable for readers of all ages.
ratings.viz.com

PERFECT SQUARE
VIZ media
www.viz.com

End papers by Sun-Min Kim and David Horvath | **"Frostbite Returns"** story by Travis Nichols, art by Ian McGinty, colors by Fred C. Stresing | **"My Hero"** story Travis Nichols, art by Phillip Jacobson, colors by Fred C. Stresing | **"Save Us"** story and art by Sun-Min Kim | **"Know Thy Enemy"** story Travis Nichols art by Ian McGinty, colors by Fred C. Stresing | **"The Twelve Heroic Types"** story and art by Travis Nichols | **"My Enemy Myself"** story by Travis Nichols, art by Phillip Jacobson, colors by Fred C. Stresings | **"Zombie Hero"** story and art by MAD BARBARIANS | **"Ugleague Assemble!"** story by Travis Nichols, art by Ian McGinty, colors by Fred C. Stresing | **"Uglylair"** art by Ian McGinty, colors by Fred C. Stresing | **"To-Fu Oyako Meets Uglydoll"** story and art by DEVILROBOTS | **"Choose Wisely"** story by Travis Nichols and Phillip Jacobson, colors by Fred C. Stresings | **"News Flash!"** story and art by Theo Ellsworth | **"Uglydolls in Pretty Fruits"** story and art by Junko Mizuno | **"Be a Hero"** story and art by Travis Nichols | **"The Uglyssey"** story by Travis Nichols, art by Phillip Jacobson, colors by Fred C. Stresing

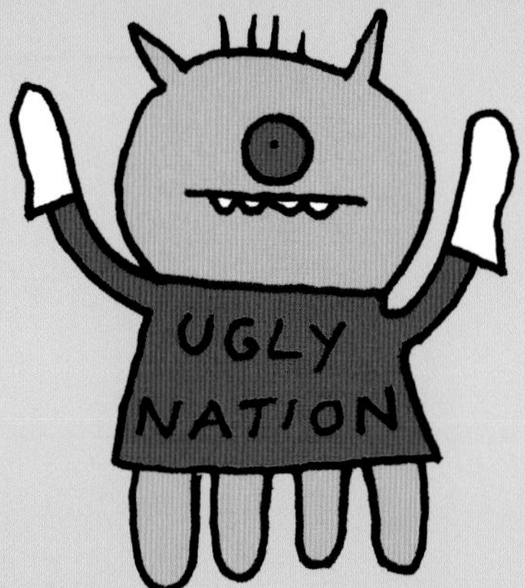

UGLY
NATION

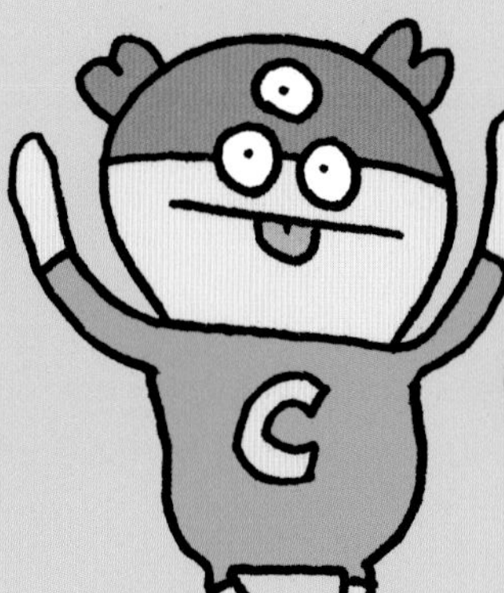

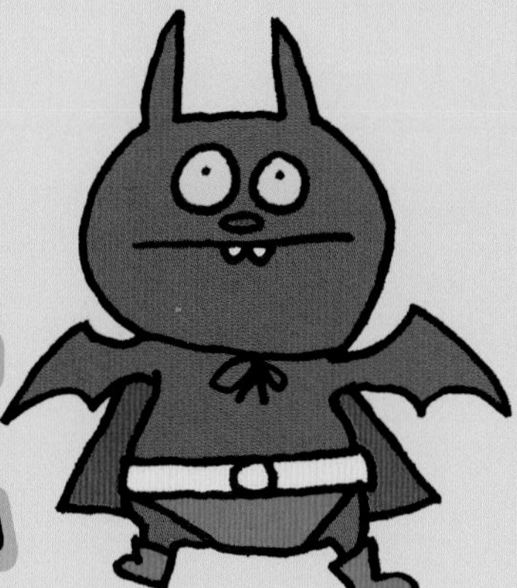

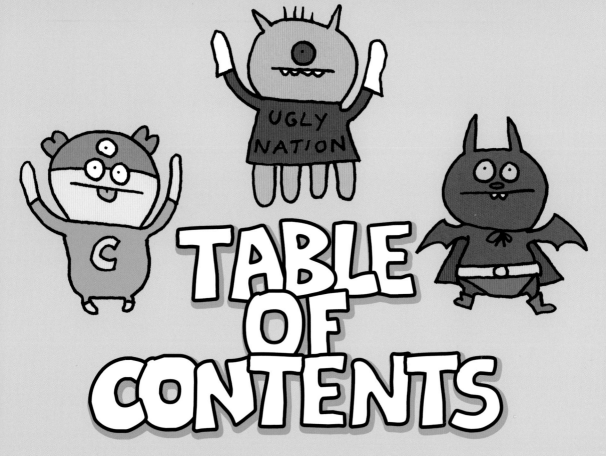

TABLE OF CONTENTS

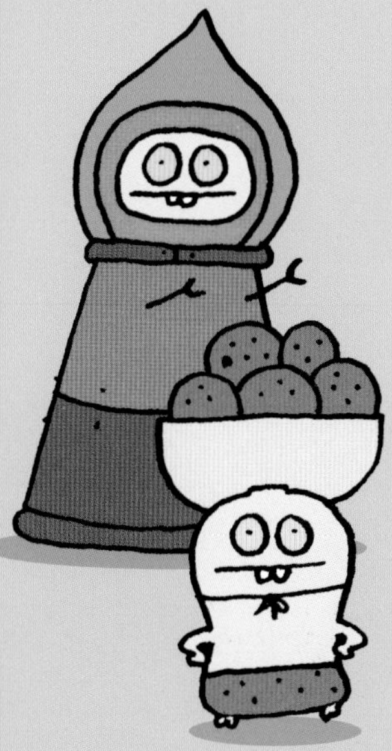

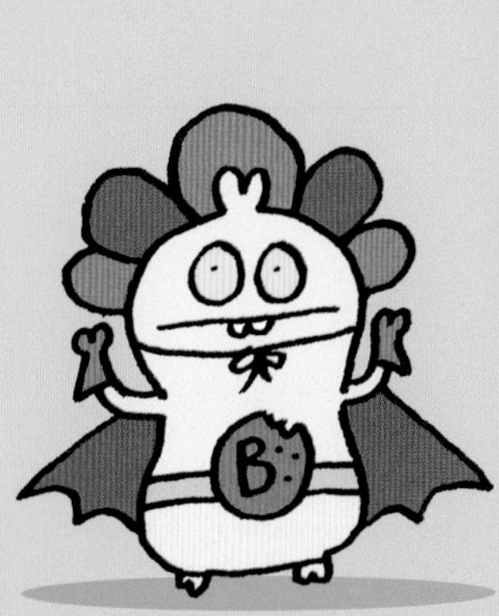

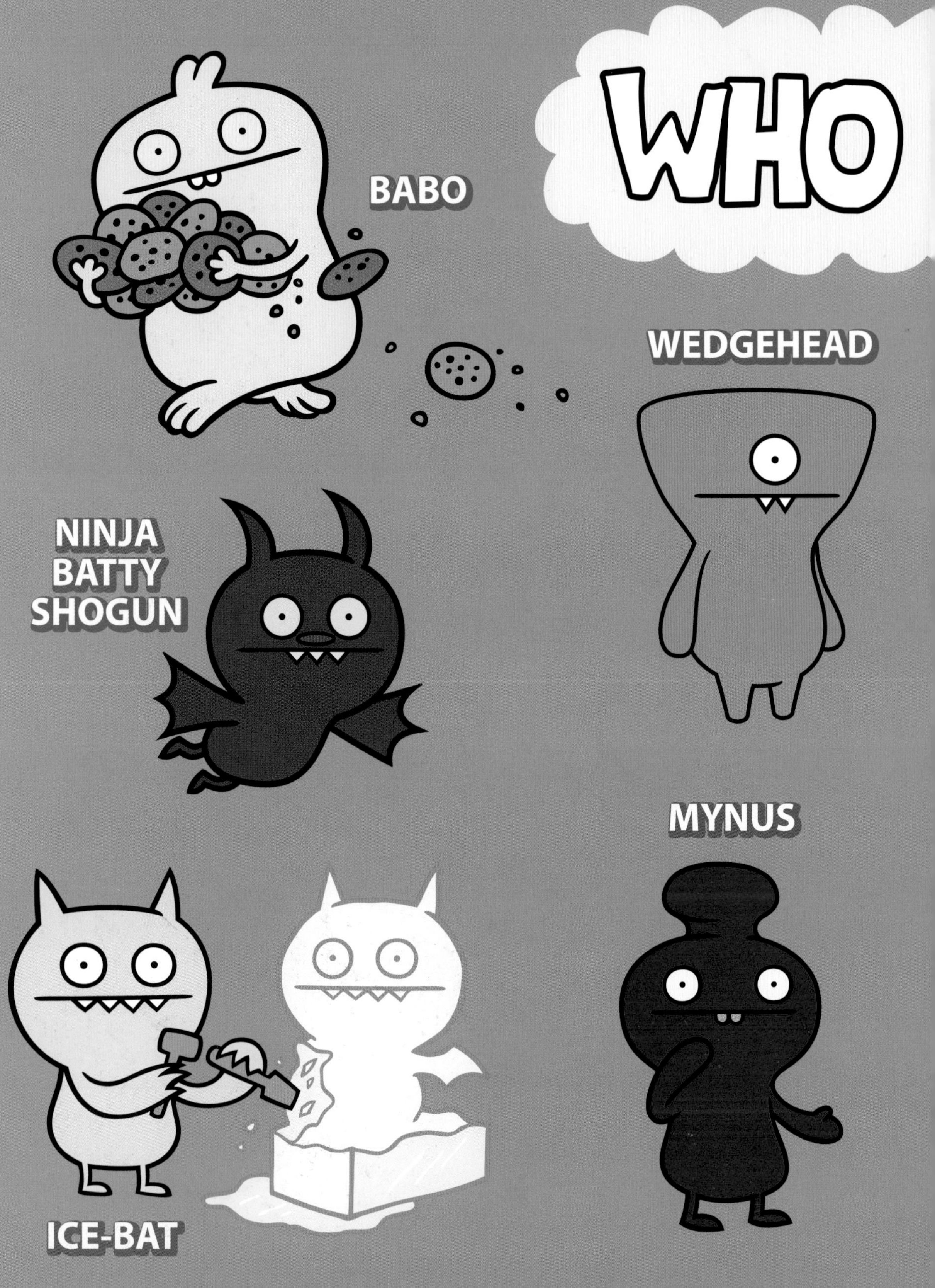
WHO
BABO
WEDGEHEAD
NINJA BATTY SHOGUN
MYNUS
ICE-BAT

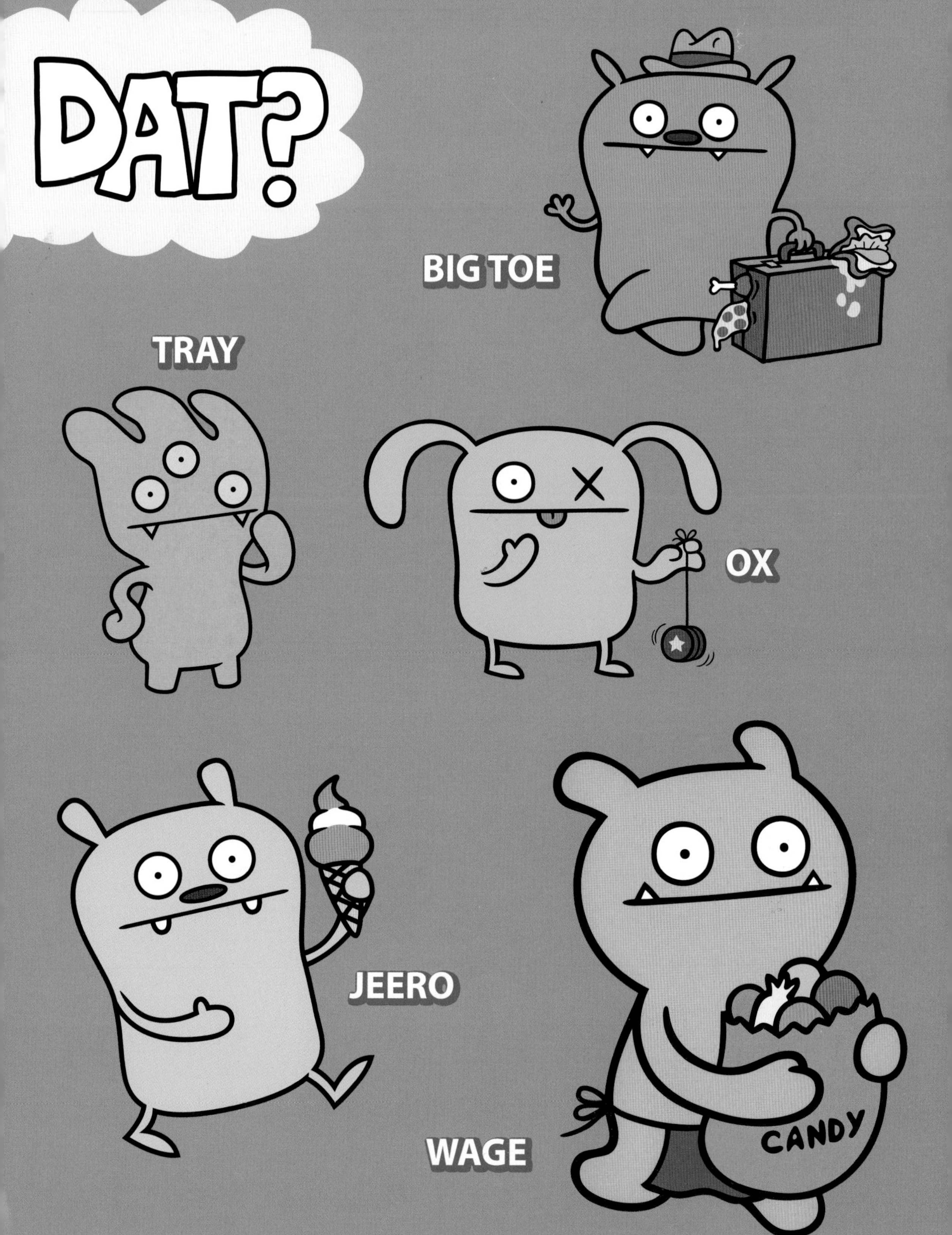
DAT?
BIG TOE
TRAY
OX
JEERO
WAGE
CANDY

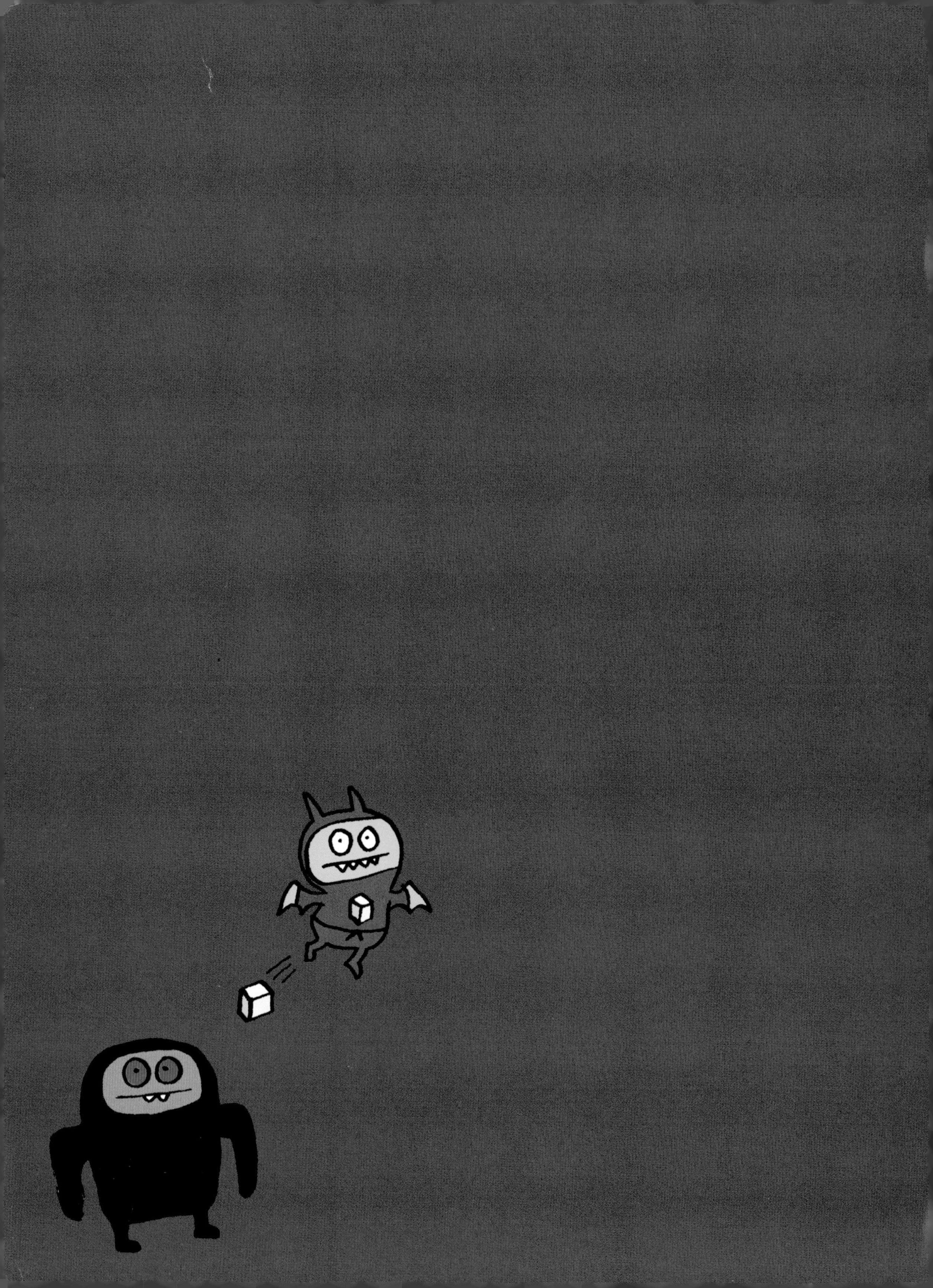

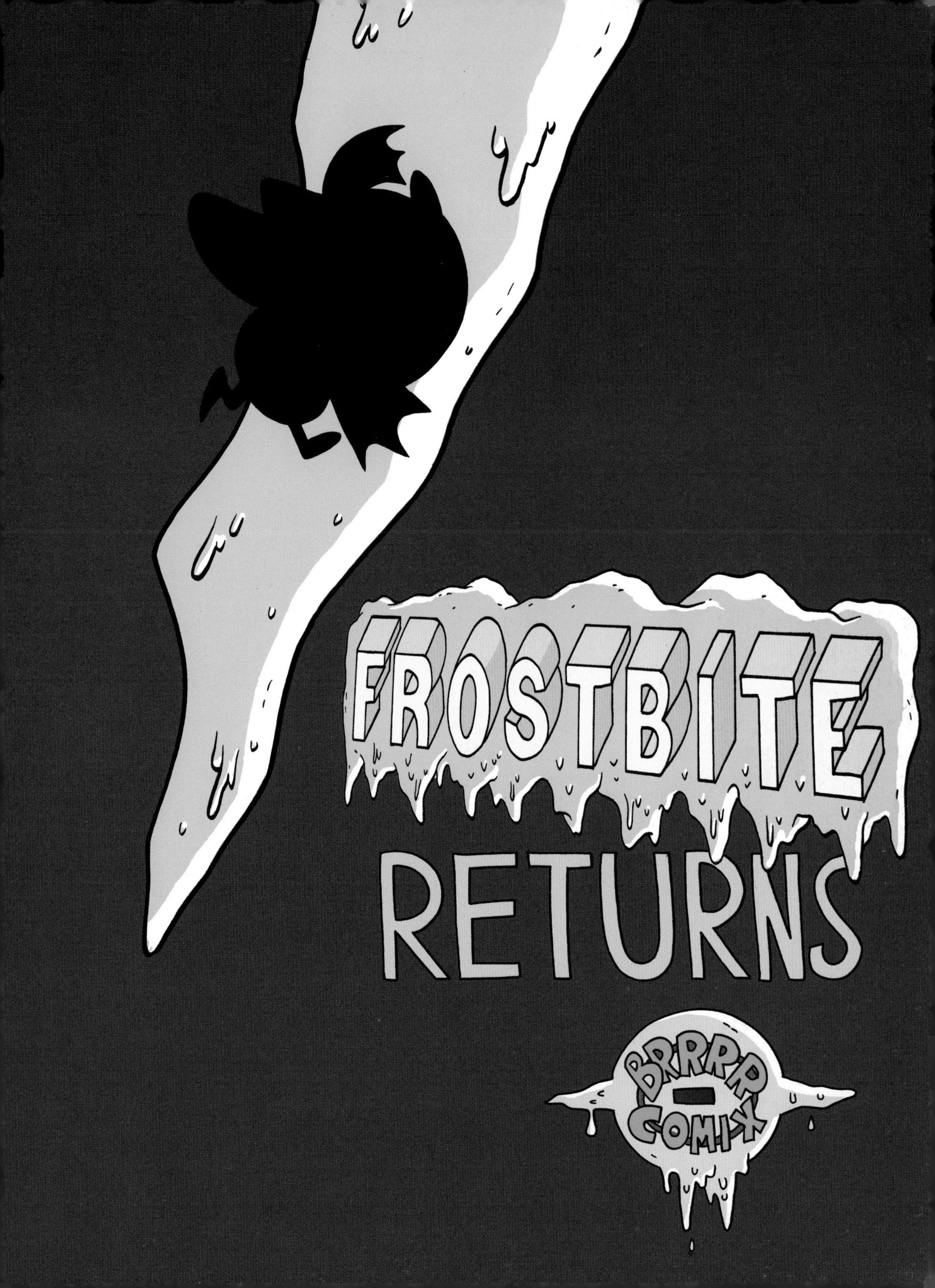
FROSTBITE
RETURNS
BRRRR
COMIX

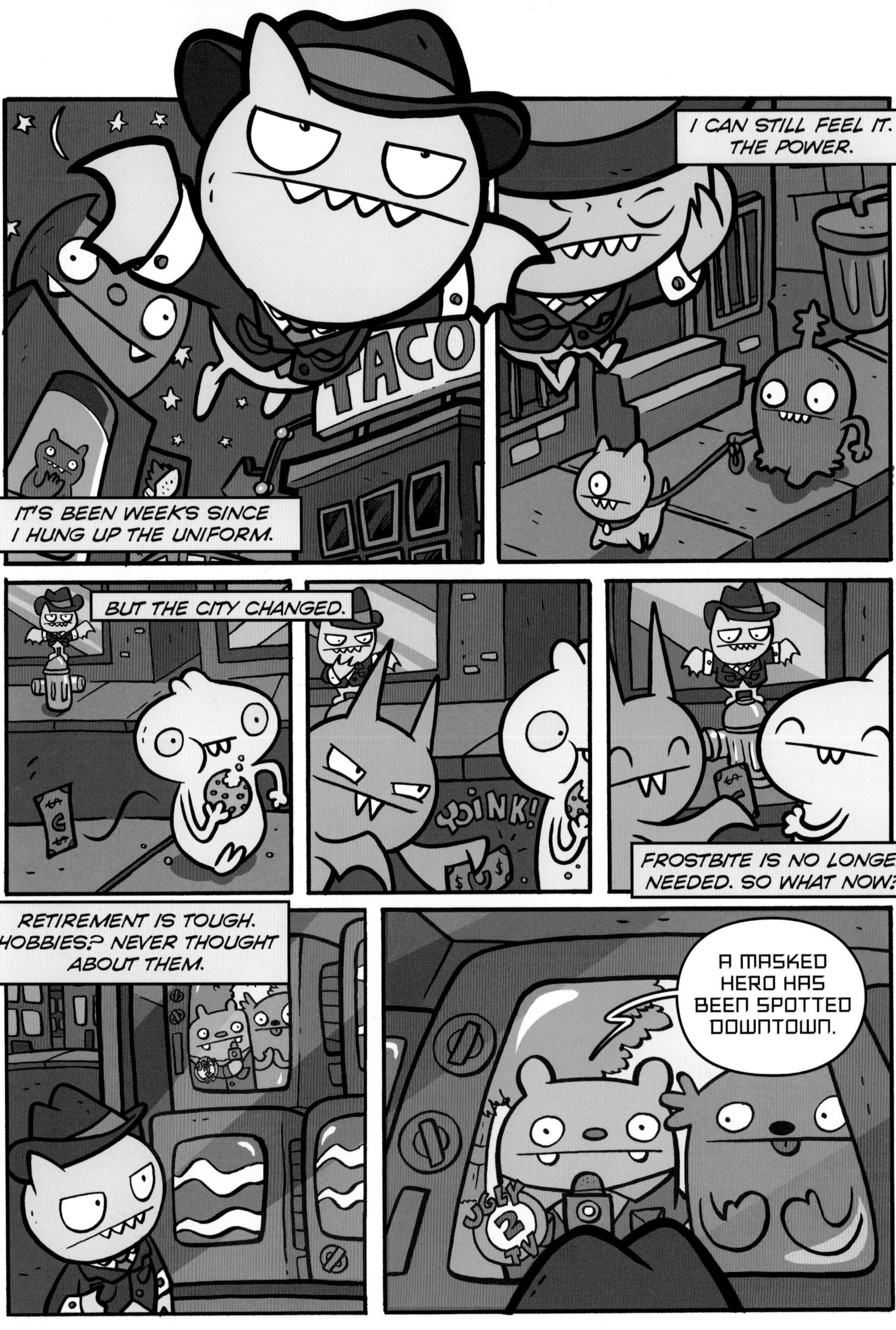

I CAN STILL FEEL IT. THE POWER.
TACO
IT'S BEEN WEEKS SINCE I HUNG UP THE UNIFORM.
BUT THE CITY CHANGED.
YOINK!
FROSTBITE IS NO LONGER NEEDED. SO WHAT NOW?
RETIREMENT IS TOUGH. HOBBIES? NEVER THOUGHT ABOUT THEM.
A MASKED HERO HAS BEEN SPOTTED DOWNTOWN.
UGLY 2 TV

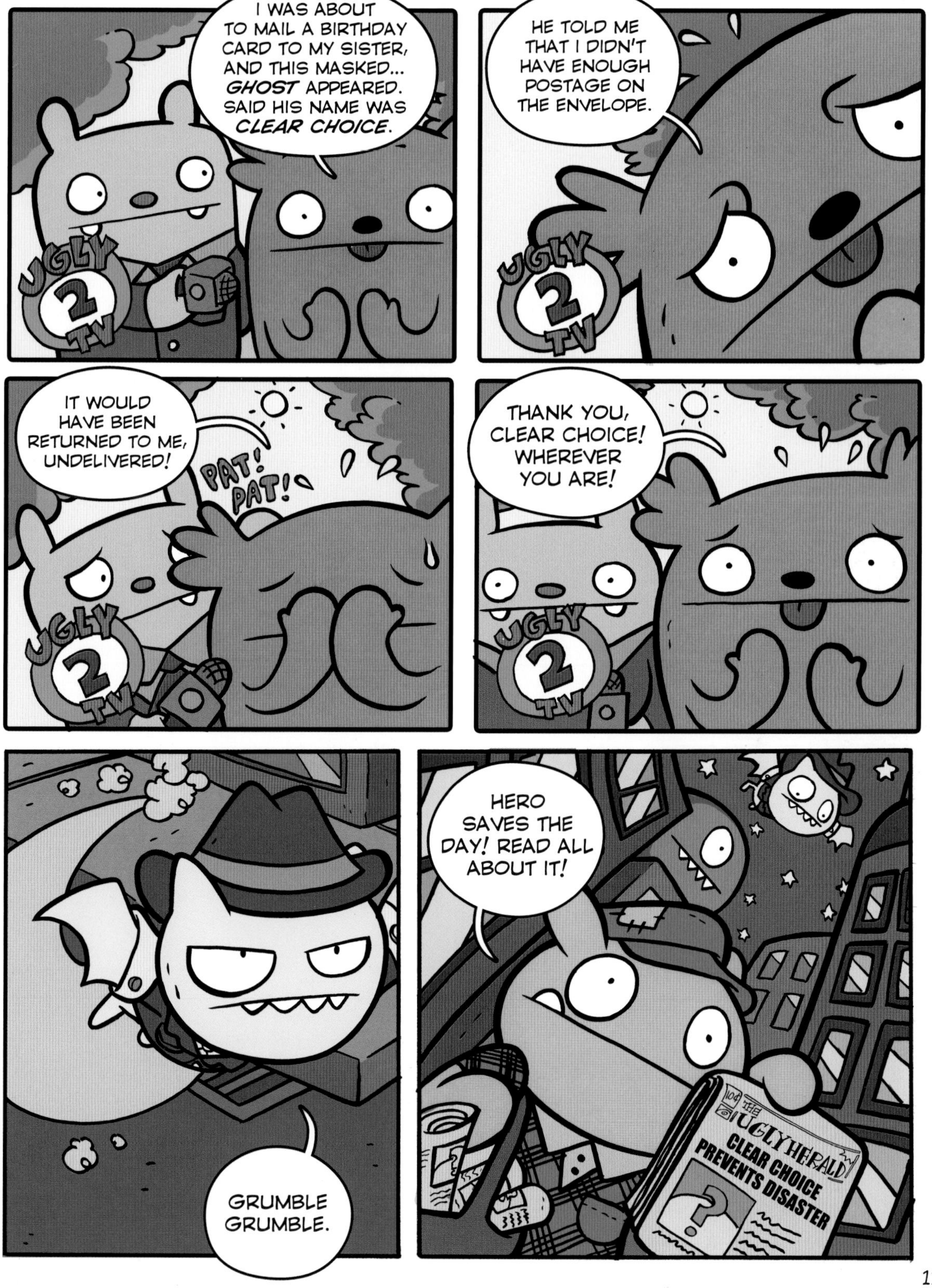
I WAS ABOUT TO MAIL A BIRTHDAY CARD TO MY SISTER, AND THIS MASKED... GHOST APPEARED. SAID HIS NAME WAS CLEAR CHOICE.
UGLY 2 TV
HE TOLD ME THAT I DIDN'T HAVE ENOUGH POSTAGE ON THE ENVELOPE.
UGLY 2 TV
IT WOULD HAVE BEEN RETURNED TO ME, UNDELIVERED!
PAT! PAT!
UGLY 2 TV
THANK YOU, CLEAR CHOICE! WHEREVER YOU ARE!
UGLY 2 TV
GRUMBLE GRUMBLE.
HERO SAVES THE DAY! READ ALL ABOUT IT!
10¢ THE UGLY HERALD
CLEAR CHOICE PREVENTS DISASTER

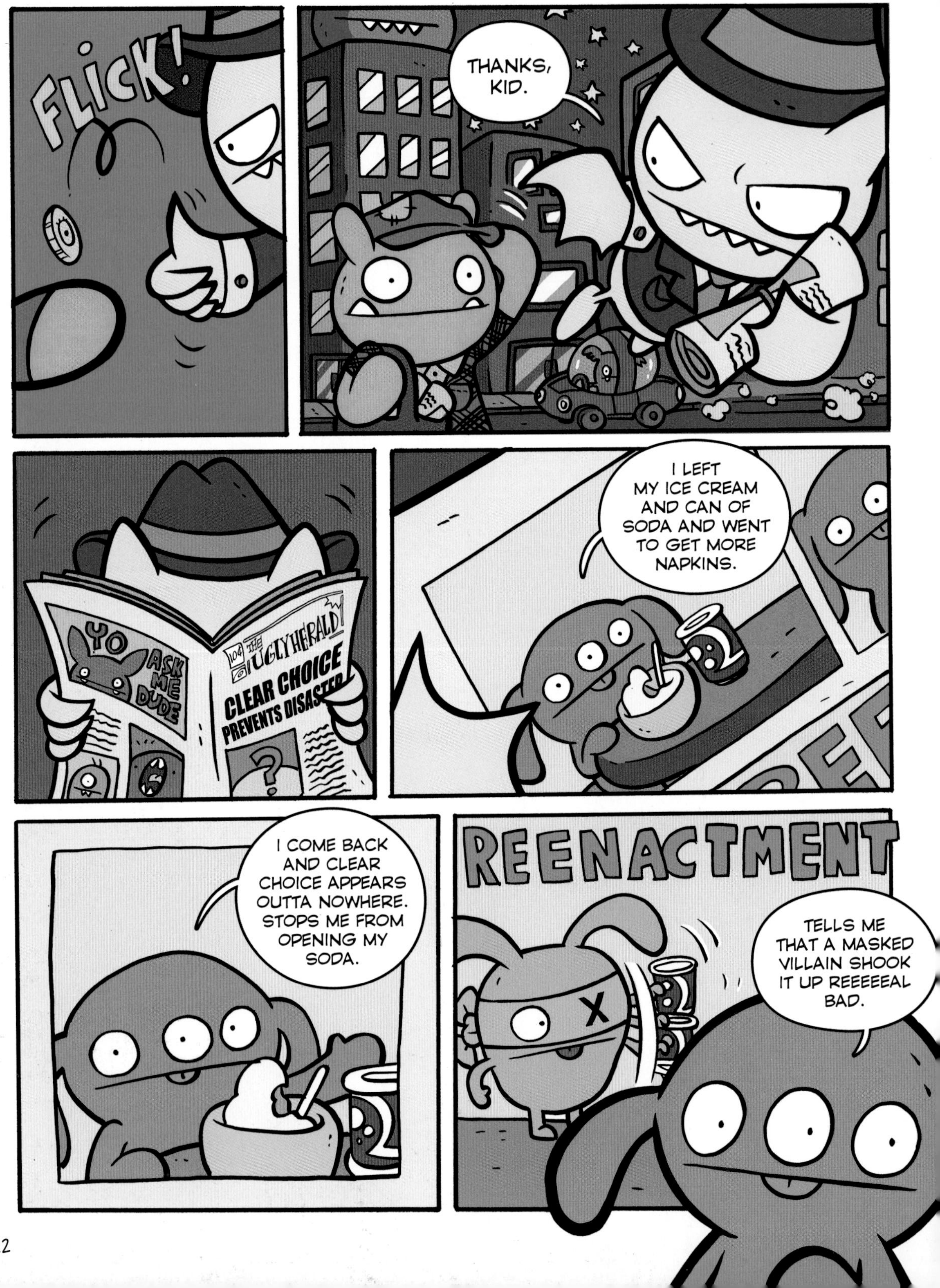
FLICK!
THANKS, KID.
YO
ASK ME DUDE
THE UGLY HERALD
104
CLEAR CHOICE PREVENTS DISASTER
I LEFT MY ICE CREAM AND CAN OF SODA AND WENT TO GET MORE NAPKINS.
I COME BACK AND CLEAR CHOICE APPEARS OUTTA NOWHERE. STOPS ME FROM OPENING MY SODA.
REENACTMENT
TELLS ME THAT A MASKED VILLAIN SHOOK IT UP REEEEEAL BAD.

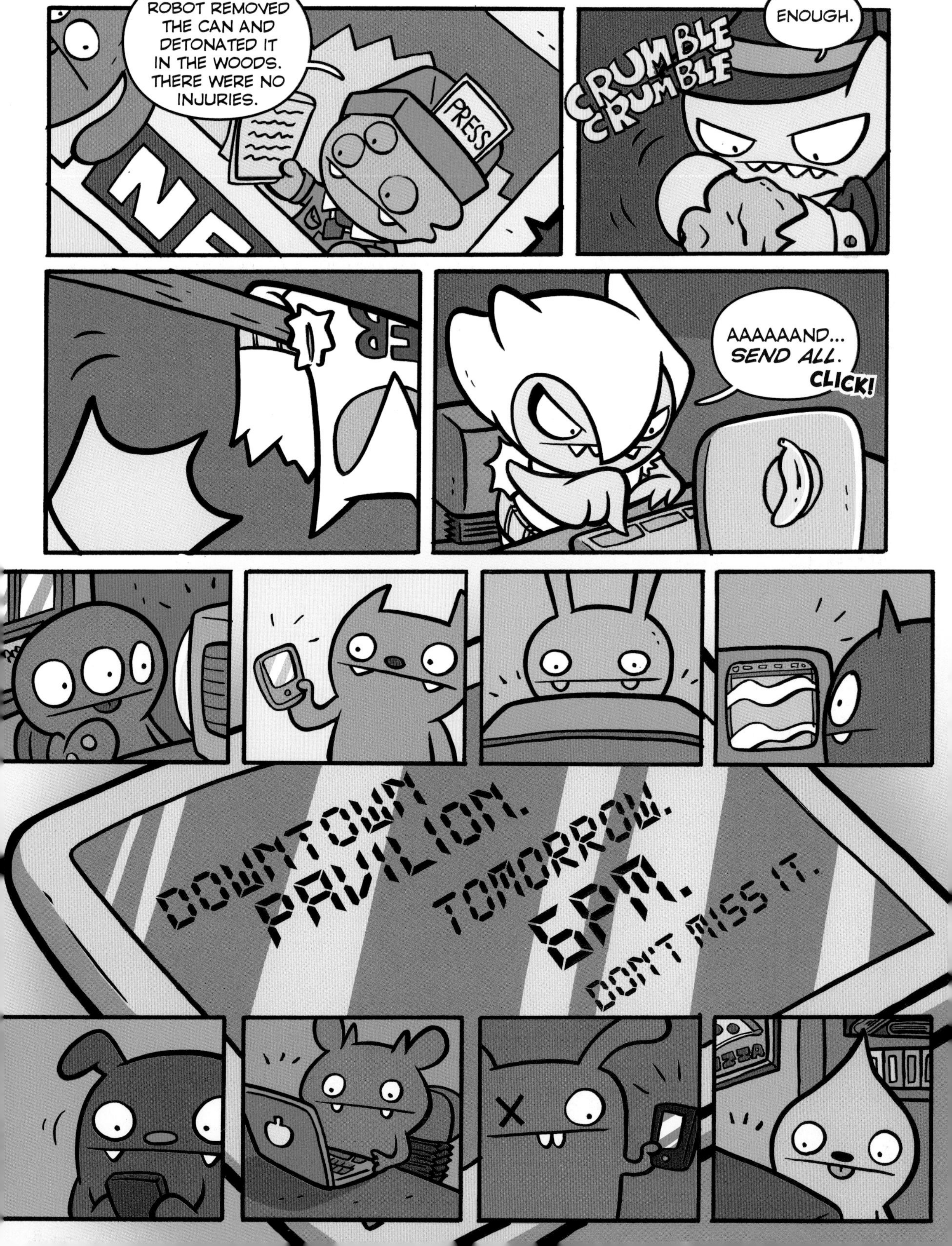
A POLICE ROBOT REMOVED THE CAN AND DETONATED IT IN THE WOODS. THERE WERE NO INJURIES.
PRESS
NE
ENOUGH.
CRUMBLE CRUMBLE
ER
AAAAAAND... SEND ALL.
CLICK!
DOWNTOWN PAVILION. TOMORROW. 6PM. DON'T MISS IT.

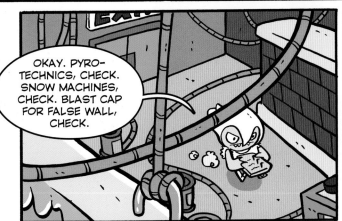

OKAY. PYRO-TECHNICS, CHECK. SNOW MACHINES, CHECK. BLAST CAP FOR FALSE WALL, CHECK.

3...
2...
1...

POOF!

HELLO, FROSTBITE.

SO, YOU'RE CLEAR CHOICE. THE "HERO" EVERYONE IS TALKING ABOUT.

FIRST OFF, I'M A *HUGE* FAN.

14

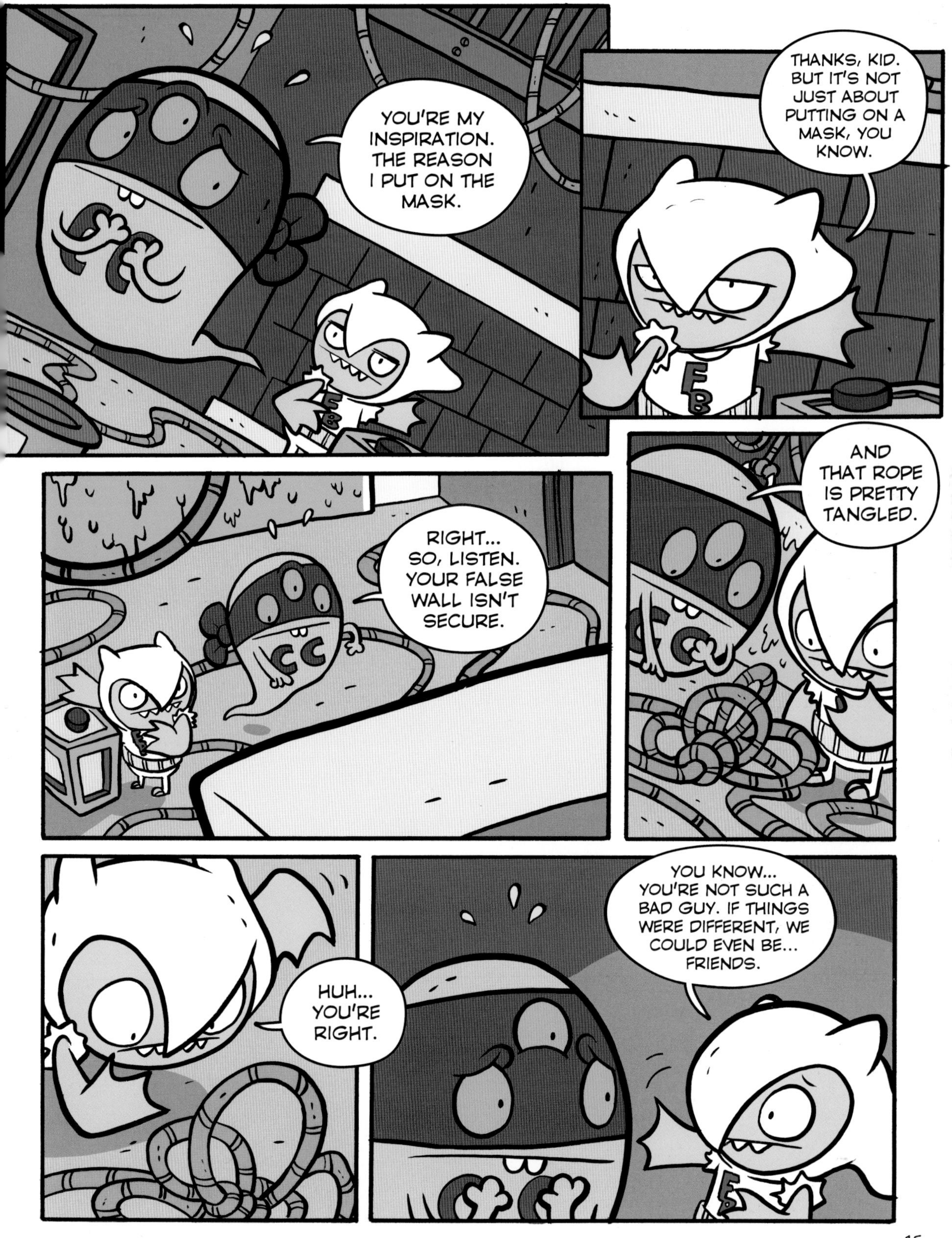
YOU'RE MY INSPIRATION. THE REASON I PUT ON THE MASK.
THANKS, KID. BUT IT'S NOT JUST ABOUT PUTTING ON A MASK, YOU KNOW.
RIGHT... SO, LISTEN. YOUR FALSE WALL ISN'T SECURE.
AND THAT ROPE IS PRETTY TANGLED.
HUH... YOU'RE RIGHT.
YOU KNOW... YOU'RE NOT SUCH A BAD GUY. IF THINGS WERE DIFFERENT, WE COULD EVEN BE... FRIENDS.

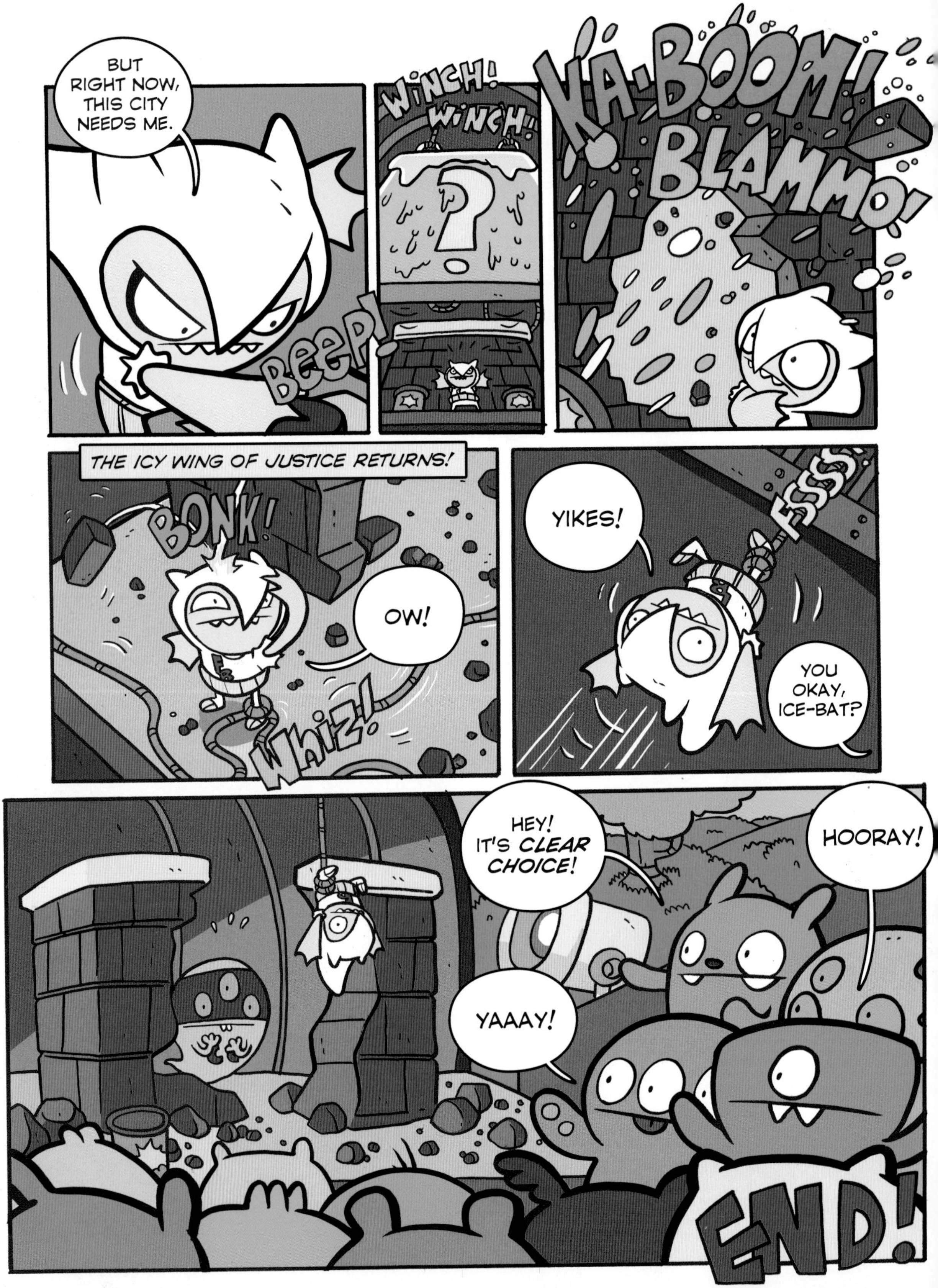
BUT RIGHT NOW, THIS CITY NEEDS ME.
BEEP!
WINCH! WINCH!
KA-BOOM! BLAMMO!
THE ICY WING OF JUSTICE RETURNS!
BONK!
OW!
WHIZ!
YIKES!
FSSS!
YOU OKAY, ICE-BAT?
HEY! IT'S *CLEAR CHOICE*!
HOORAY!
YAAAY!
END!

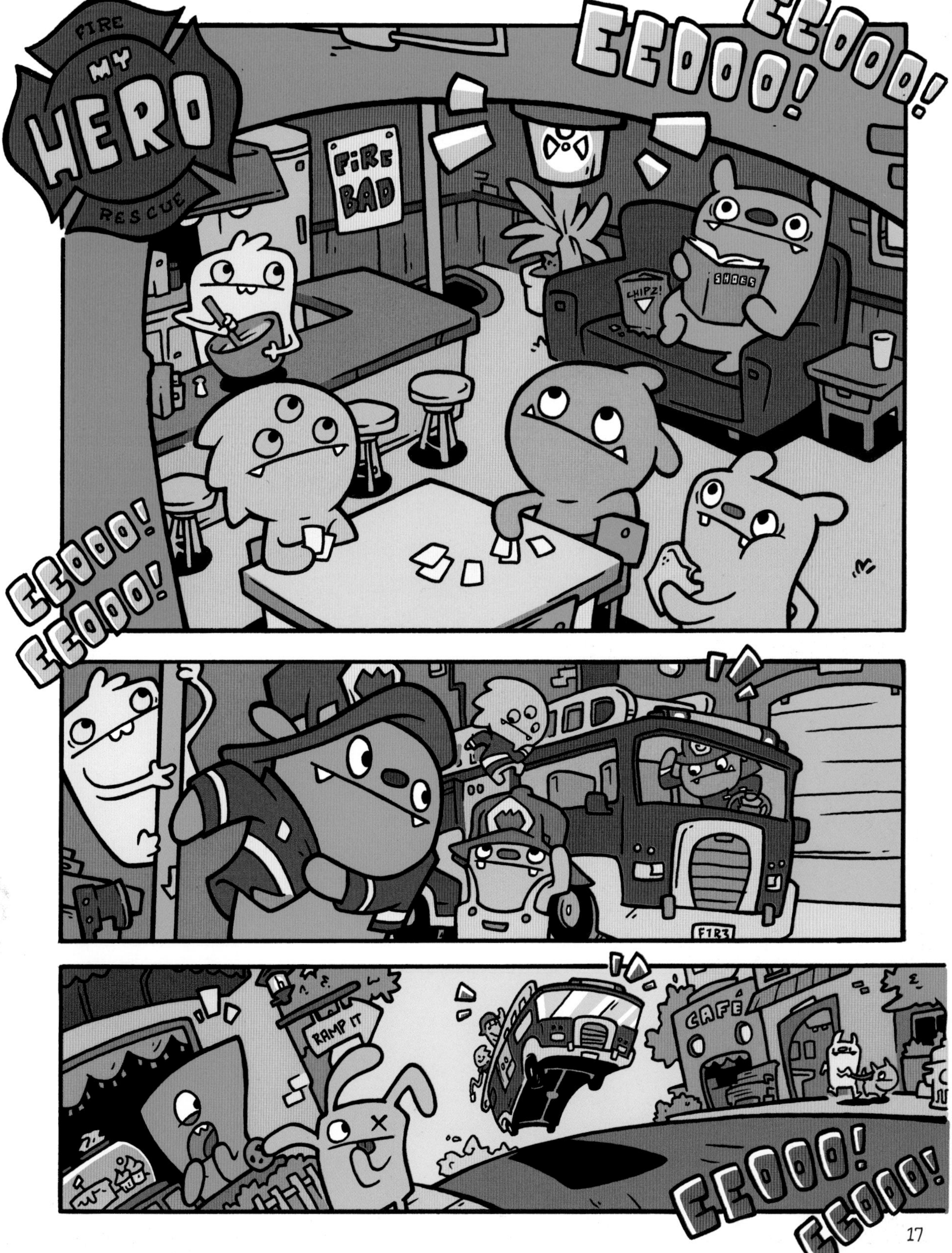
FIRE
MY
HERO
RESCUE
EEOOO! EEOOO!
FIRE BAD
CHIPZ!
SHOES
EEOOO! EEOOO!
F1R3
RAMP IT
CAFE
EEOOO! EEOOO!

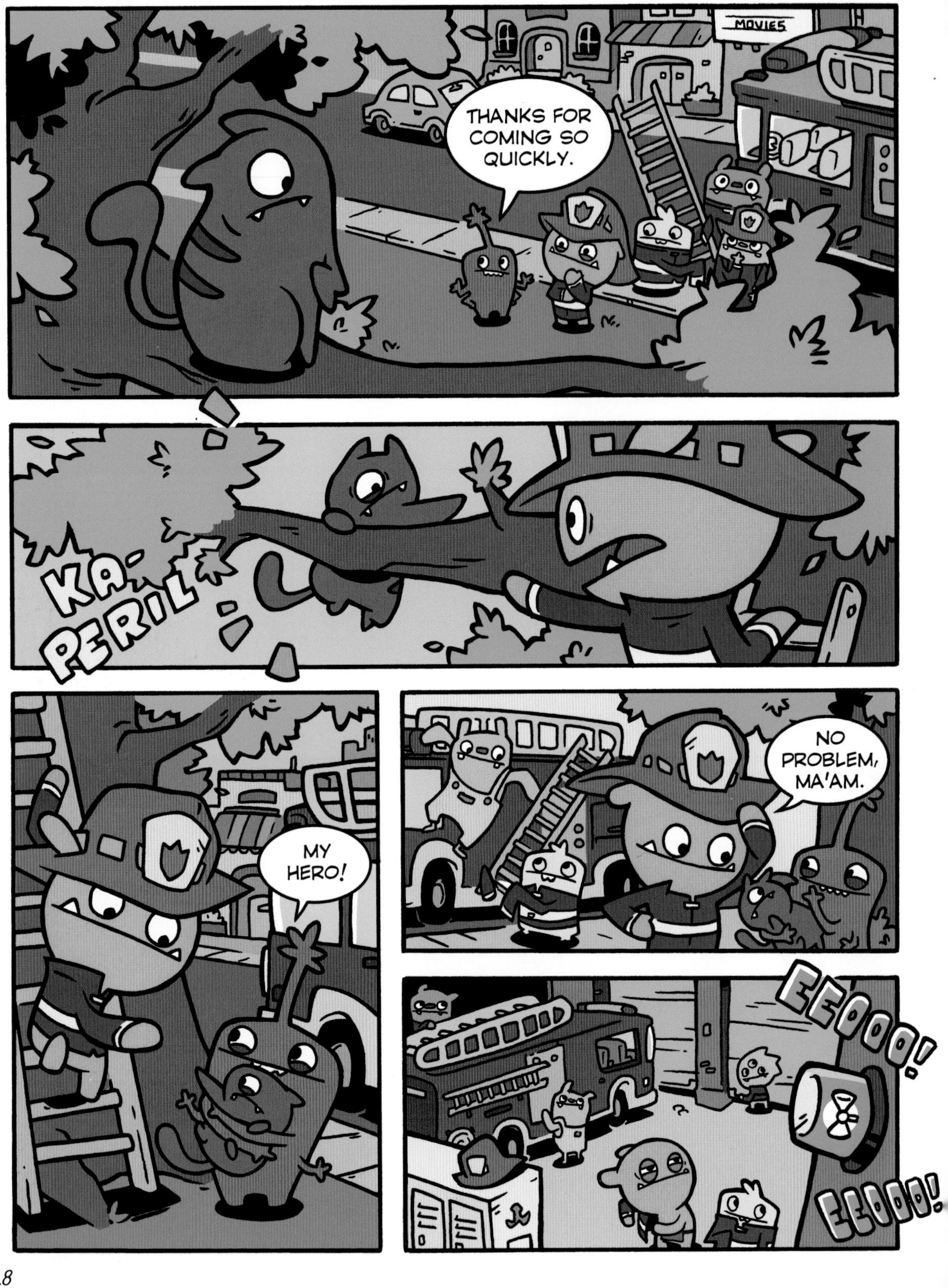
MOVIES
THANKS FOR COMING SO QUICKLY.
KA-PERIL
MY HERO!
NO PROBLEM, MA'AM.
EEOOO!
EEOOO!

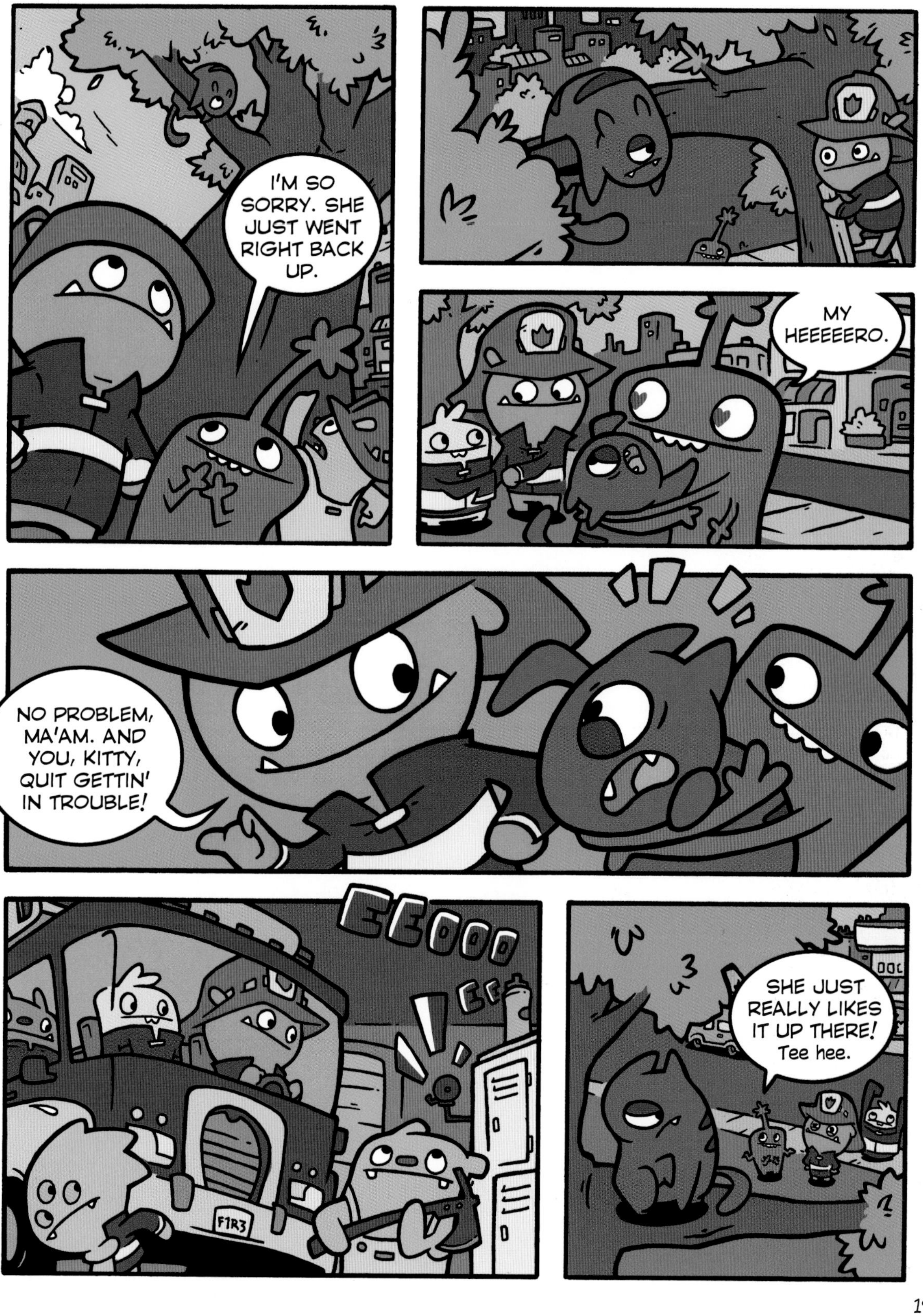
I'M SO SORRY. SHE JUST WENT RIGHT BACK UP.
MY HEEEEERO.
NO PROBLEM, MA'AM. AND YOU, KITTY, QUIT GETTIN' IN TROUBLE!
EEOOOO
EE
F1R3
SHE JUST REALLY LIKES IT UP THERE! Tee hee.

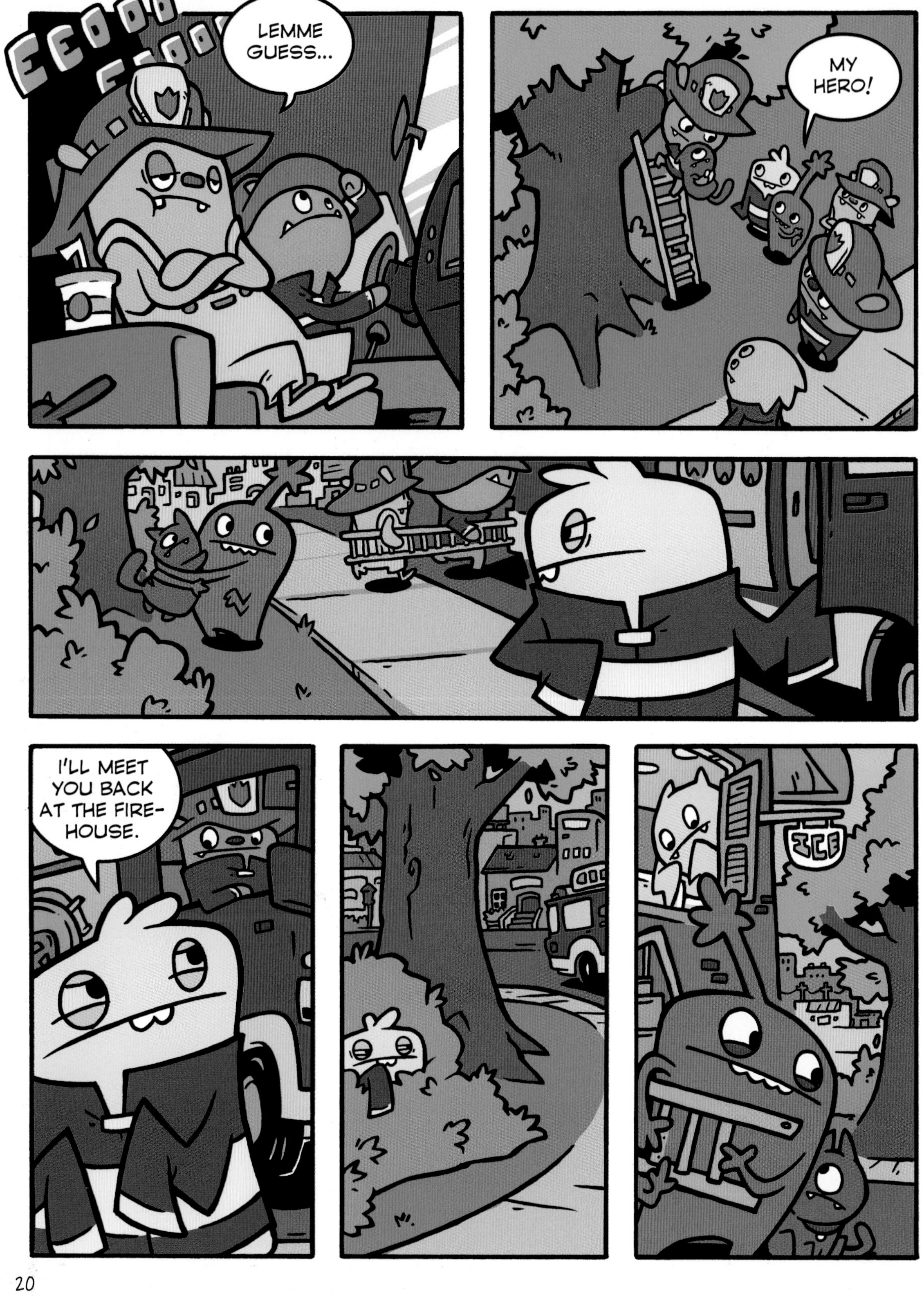
EEOOO
LEMME GUESS...
MY HERO!
I'LL MEET YOU BACK AT THE FIRE-HOUSE.
ICE

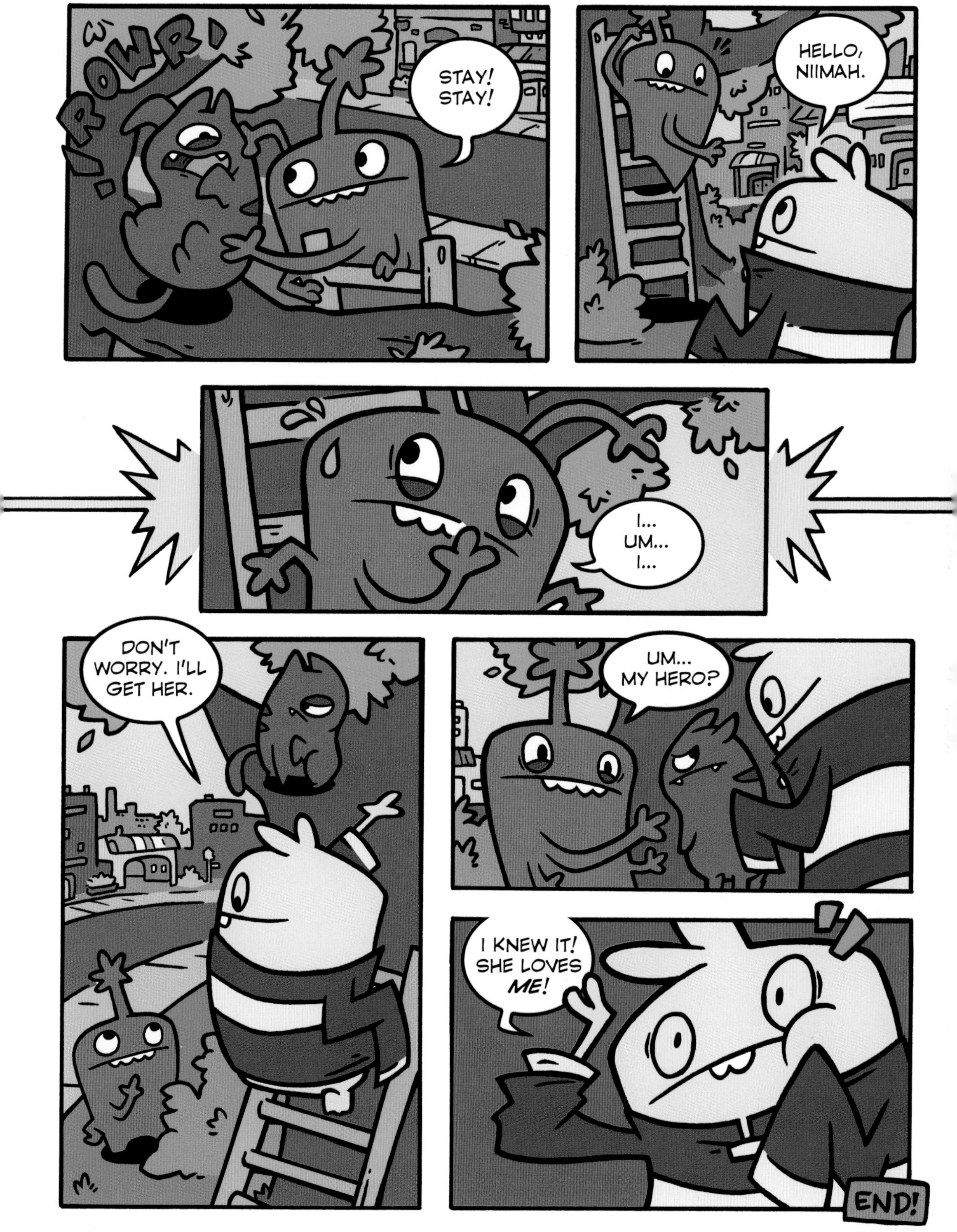
ROWR!
STAY! STAY!
HELLO, NIIMAH.
I... UM... I...
DON'T WORRY. I'LL GET HER.
UM... MY HERO?
I KNEW IT! SHE LOVES *ME*!
END!

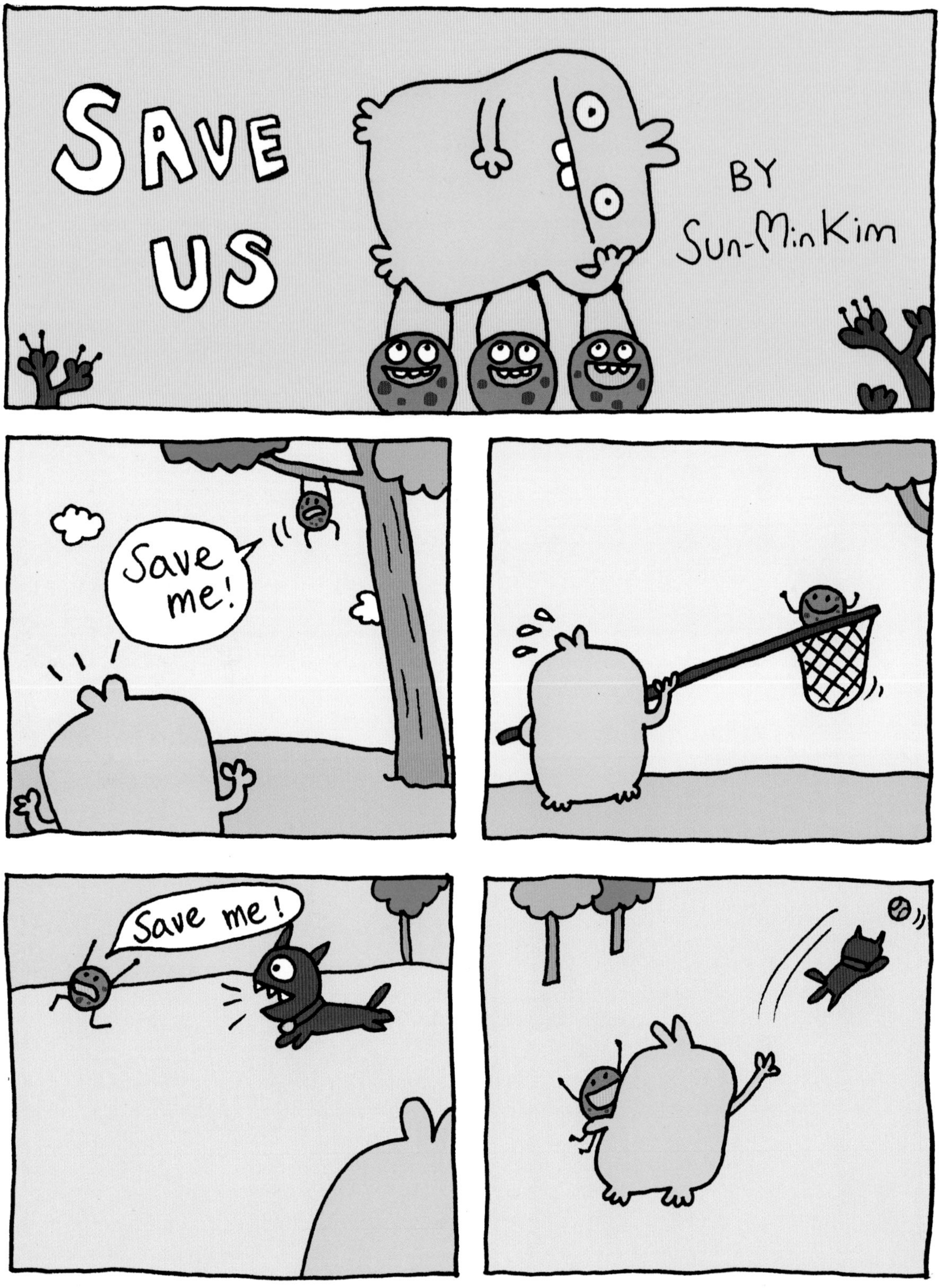
SAVE US
BY Sun-Min Kim
Save me!
Save me!

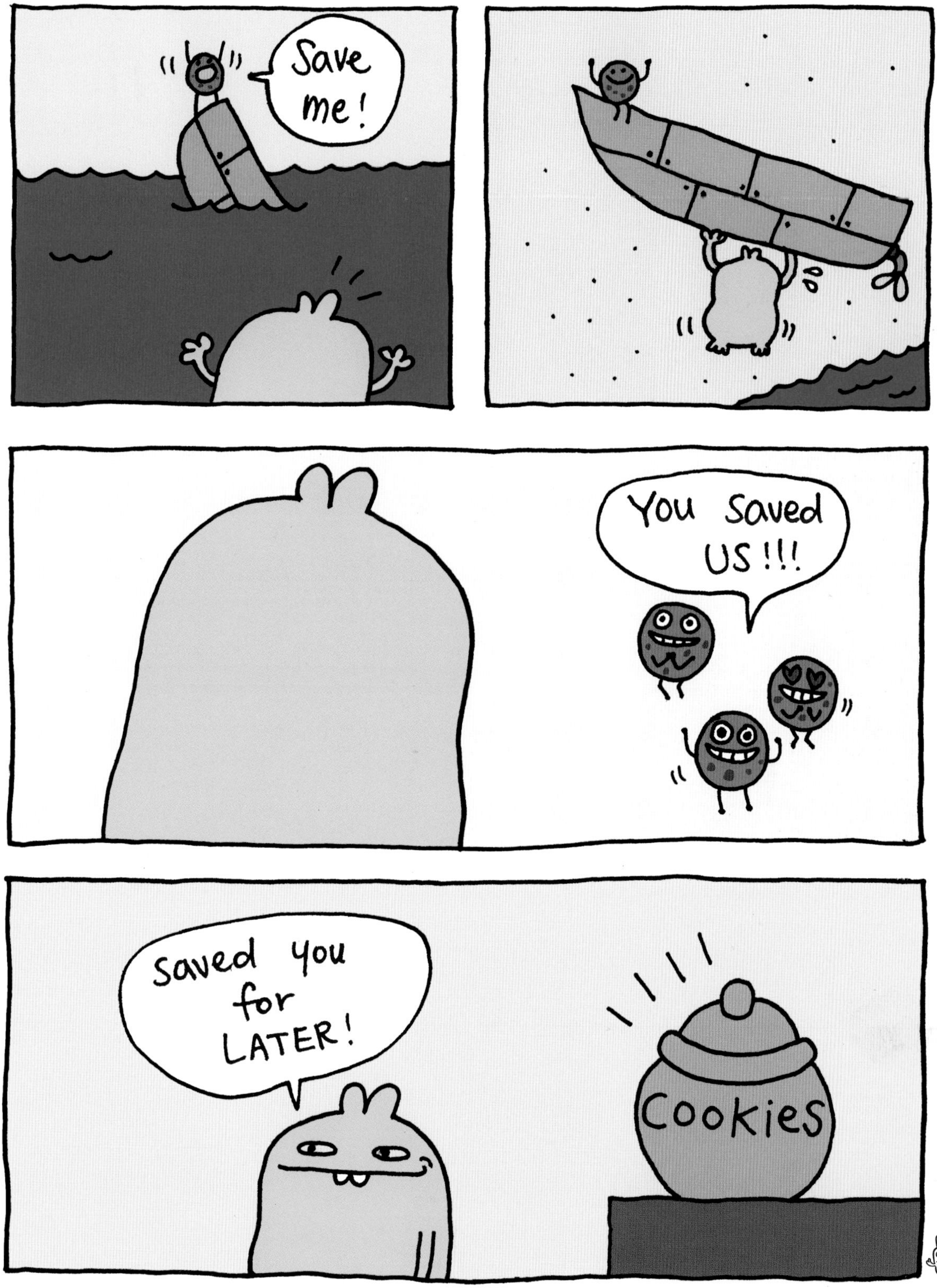
Save me!
You saved US!!!
saved you for LATER!
Cookies

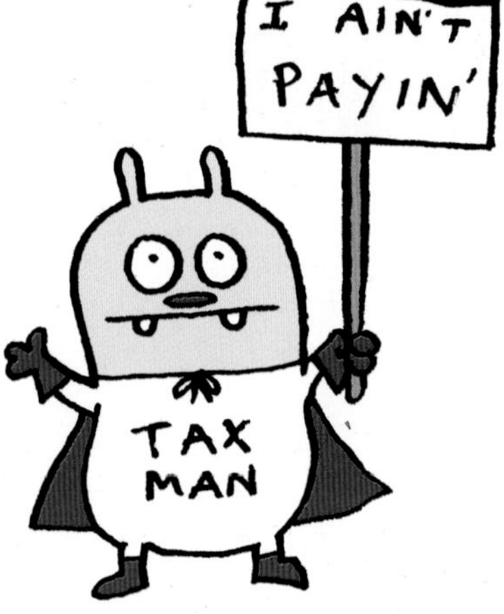
I AIN'T PAYIN'
TAX MAN

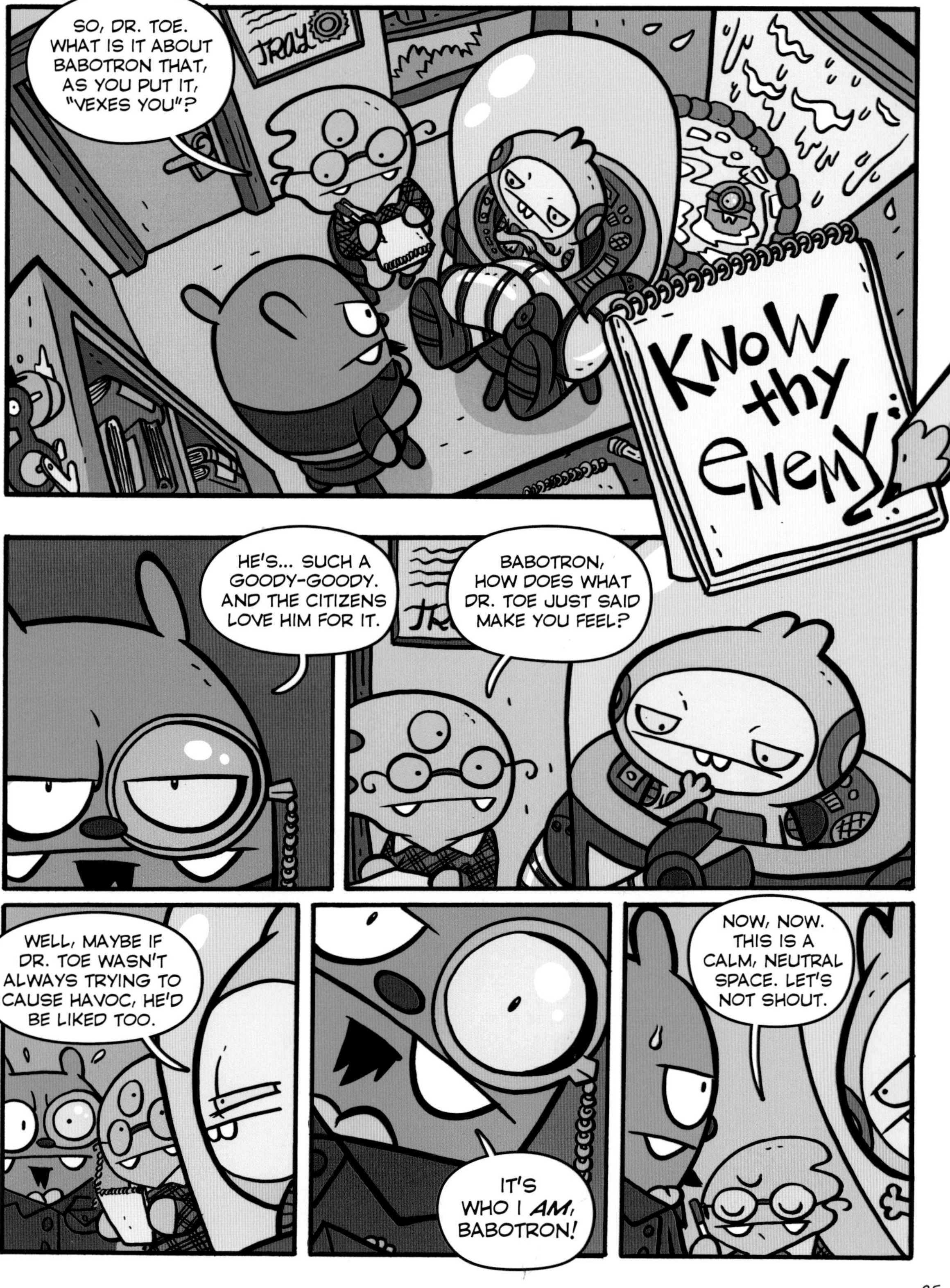
SO, DR. TOE. WHAT IS IT ABOUT BABOTRON THAT, AS YOU PUT IT, "VEXES YOU"?
TRAY
KNOW thy ENEMY
HE'S... SUCH A GOODY-GOODY. AND THE CITIZENS LOVE HIM FOR IT.
BABOTRON, HOW DOES WHAT DR. TOE JUST SAID MAKE YOU FEEL?
WELL, MAYBE IF DR. TOE WASN'T ALWAYS TRYING TO CAUSE HAVOC, HE'D BE LIKED TOO.
IT'S WHO I *AM*, BABOTRON!
NOW, NOW. THIS IS A CALM, NEUTRAL SPACE. LET'S NOT SHOUT.

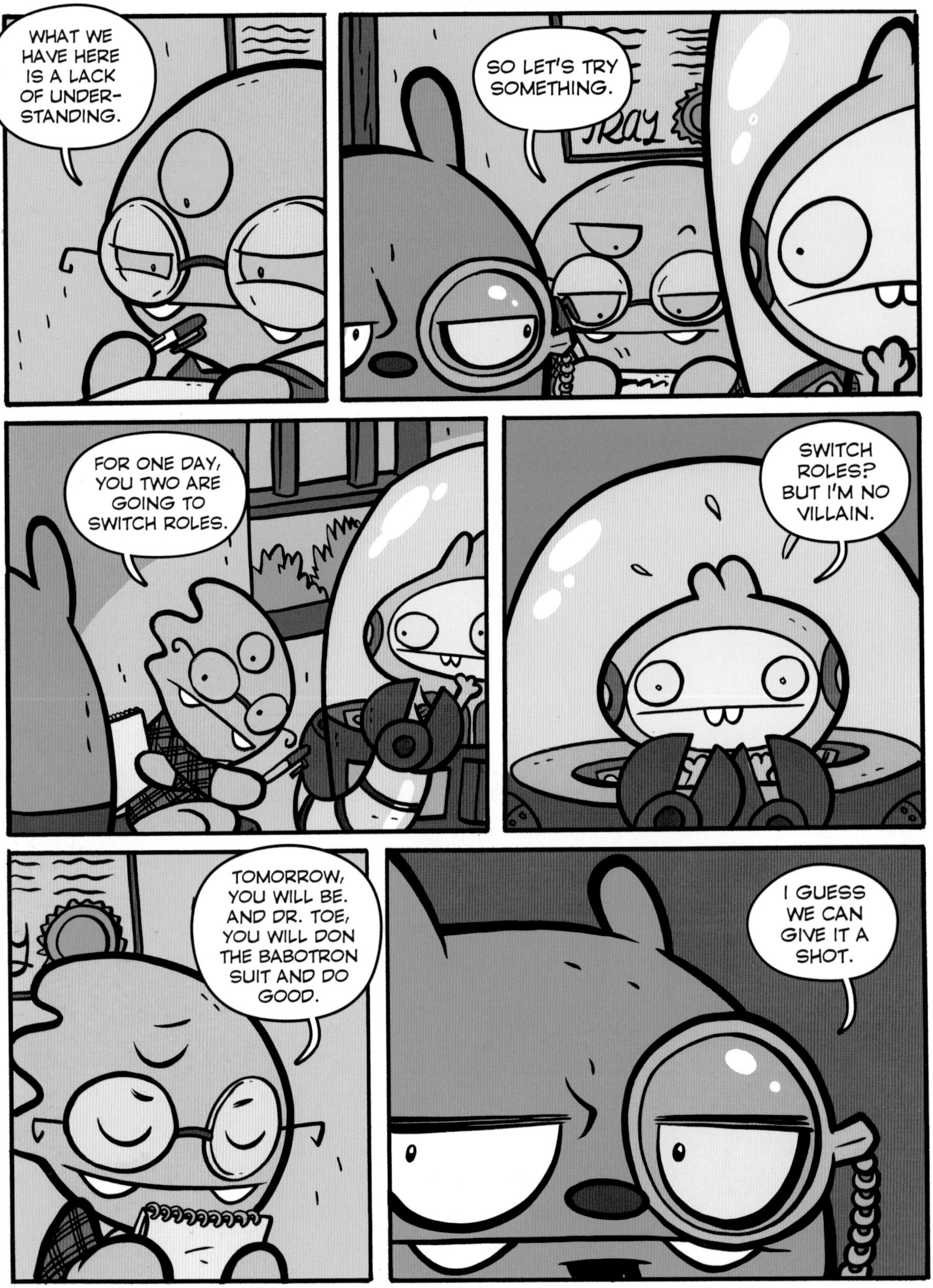
WHAT WE HAVE HERE IS A LACK OF UNDER-STANDING.
SO LET'S TRY SOMETHING.
FOR ONE DAY, YOU TWO ARE GOING TO SWITCH ROLES.
SWITCH ROLES? BUT I'M NO VILLAIN.
TOMORROW, YOU WILL BE. AND DR. TOE, YOU WILL DON THE BABOTRON SUIT AND DO GOOD.
I GUESS WE CAN GIVE IT A SHOT.

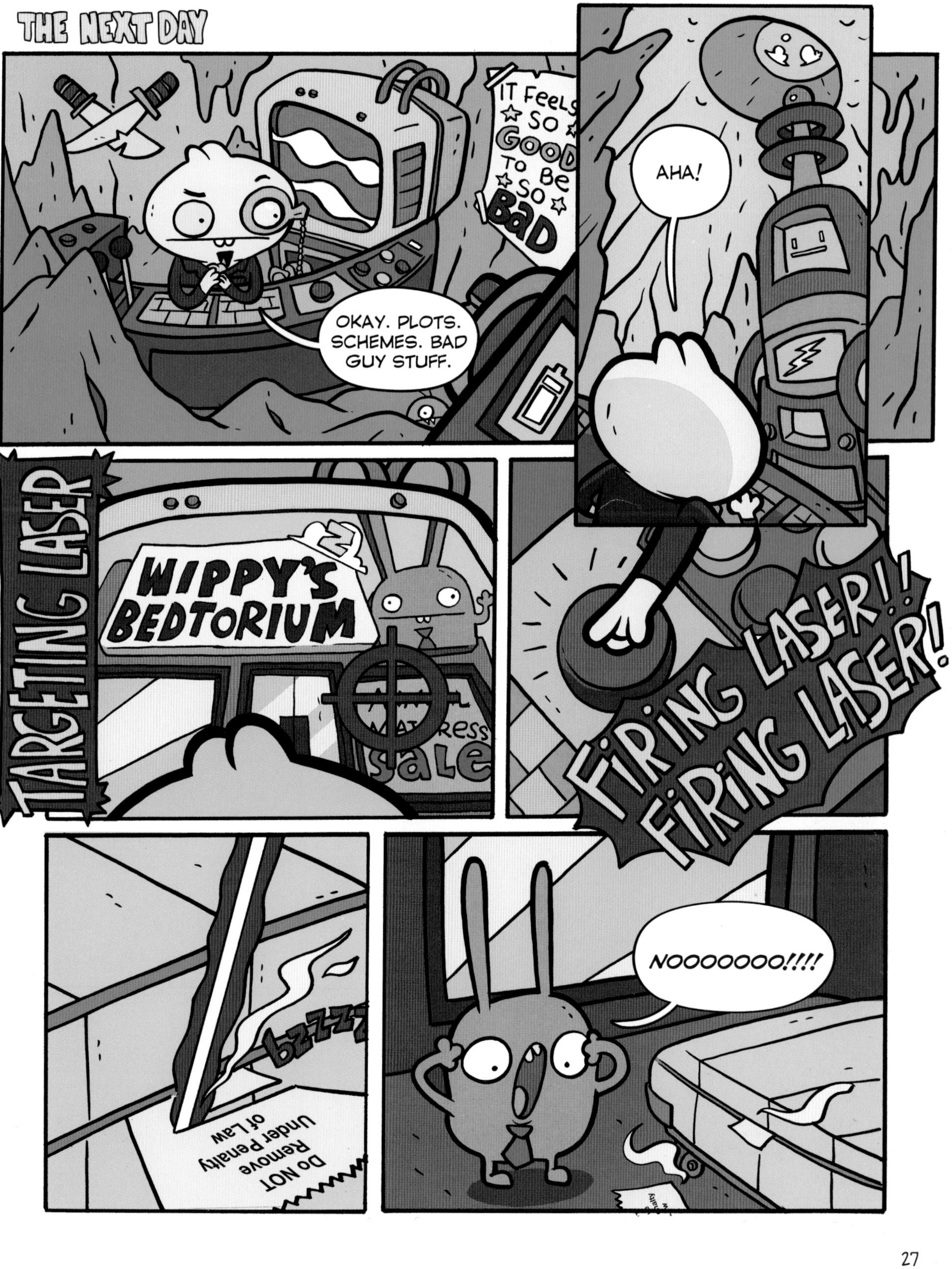
THE NEXT DAY
IT Feels So Good To Be So BAD
OKAY. PLOTS. SCHEMES. BAD GUY STUFF.
AHA!
TARGETING LASER
WIPPY'S BEDTORIUM
FIRING LASER!! FIRING LASER!
Do NOT Remove Under Penalty of Law
NOOOOOOO!!!!

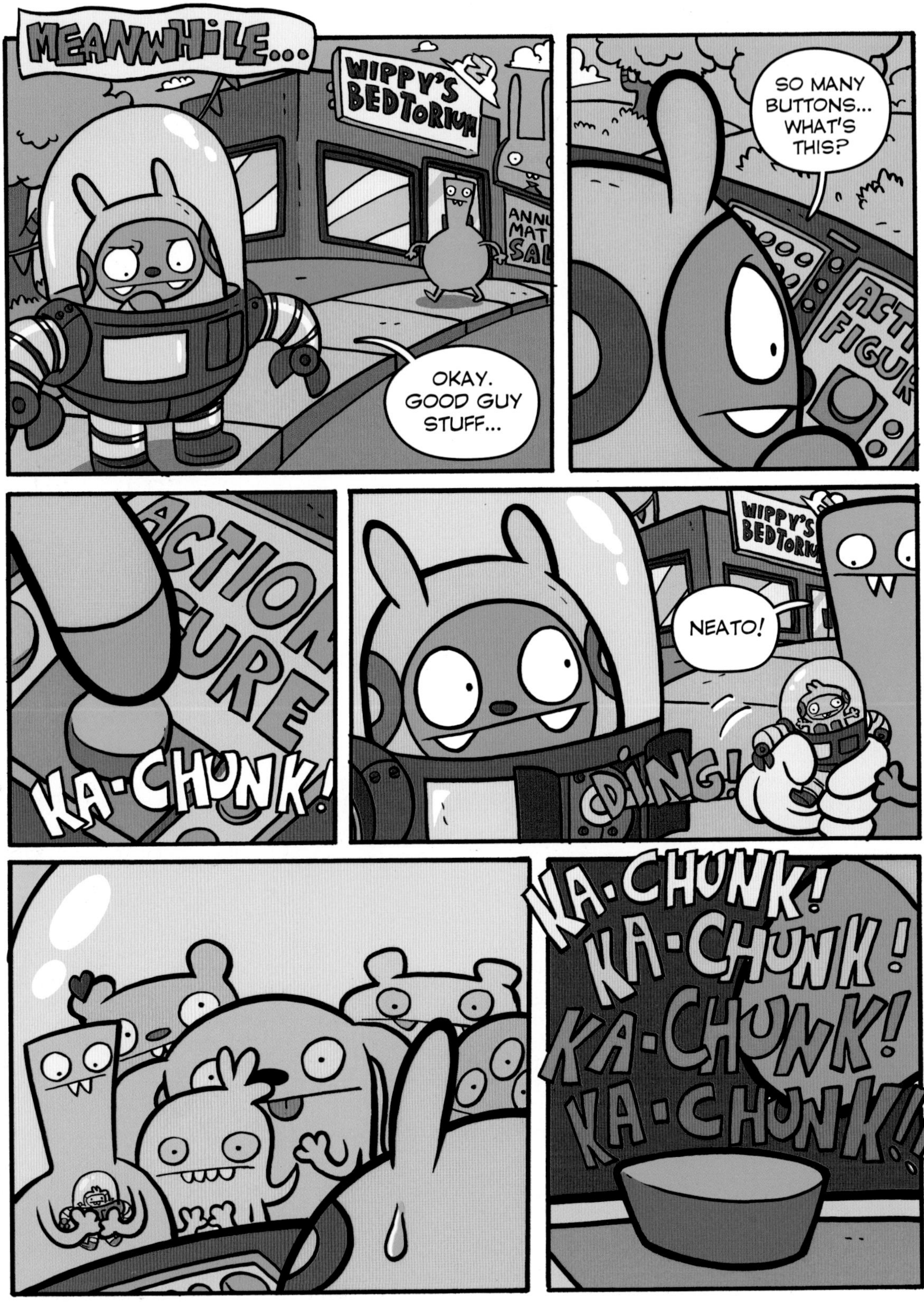
MEANWHILE...
WIPPY'S BEDTORIUM
ANNU MAT SAL
OKAY. GOOD GUY STUFF...
SO MANY BUTTONS... WHAT'S THIS?
ACTI FIGUR
ACTION FIGURE
KA-CHUNK!
WIPPY'S BEDTORIUM
NEATO!
DING!
KA-CHUNK!
KA-CHUNK!
KA-CHUNK!
KA-CHUNK!!!

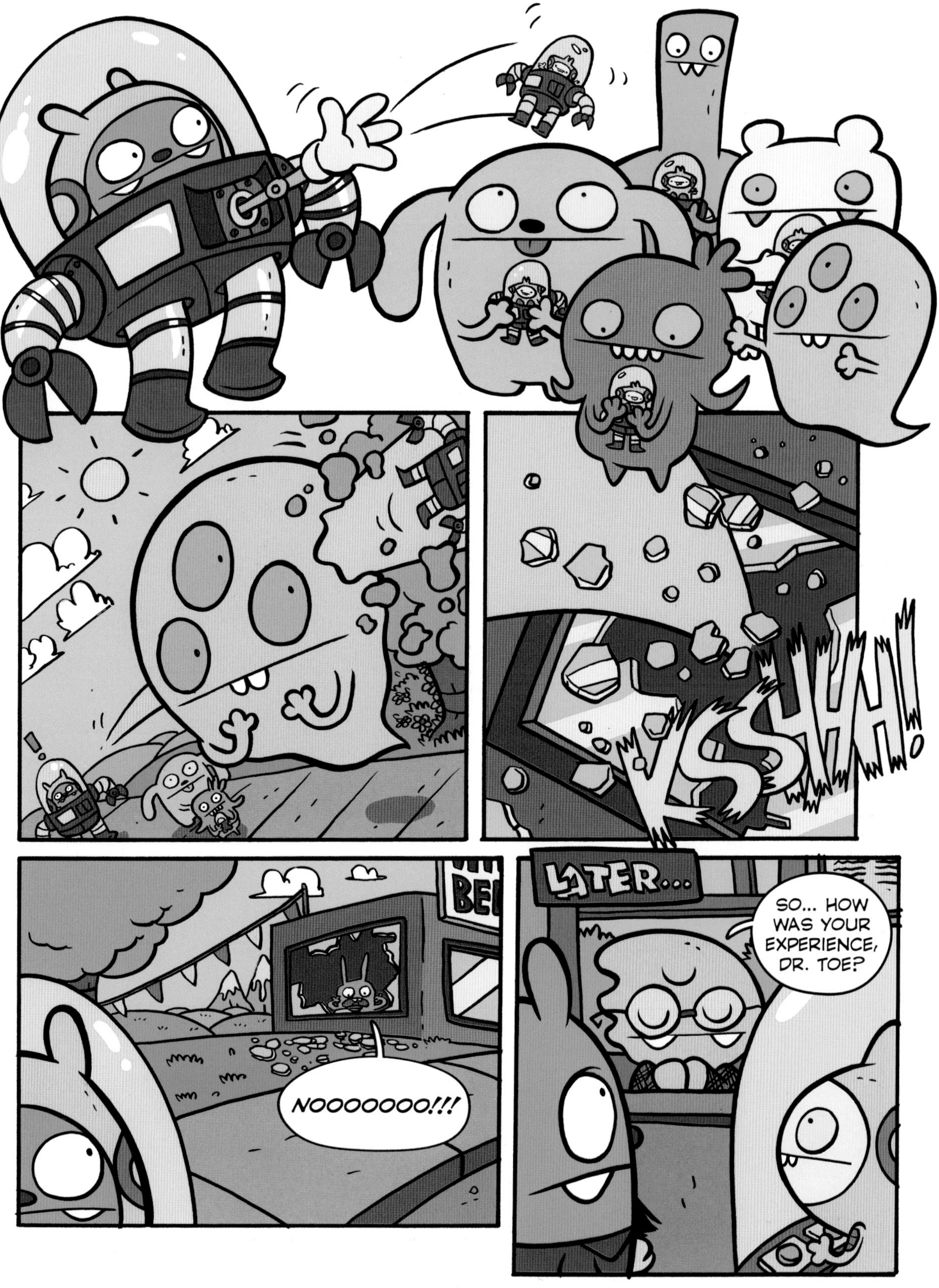
!
KSSHH!
LATER...
NOOOOOOO!!!
SO... HOW WAS YOUR EXPERIENCE, DR. TOE?

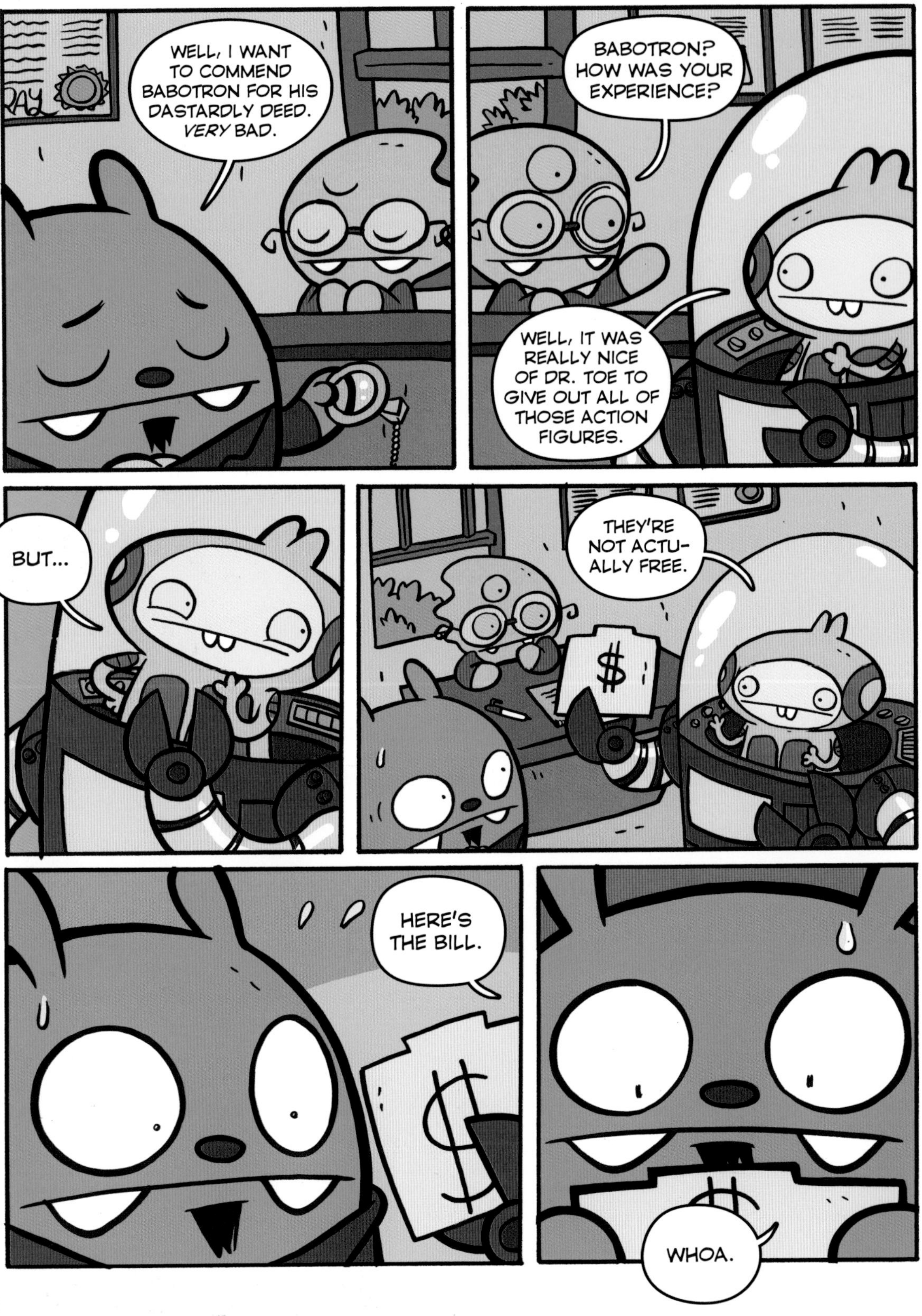

WELL, I WANT TO COMMEND BABOTRON FOR HIS DASTARDLY DEED. *VERY* BAD.
BABOTRON? HOW WAS YOUR EXPERIENCE?
WELL, IT WAS REALLY NICE OF DR. TOE TO GIVE OUT ALL OF THOSE ACTION FIGURES.
BUT...
THEY'RE NOT ACTU-ALLY FREE.
$
HERE'S THE BILL.
WHOA.

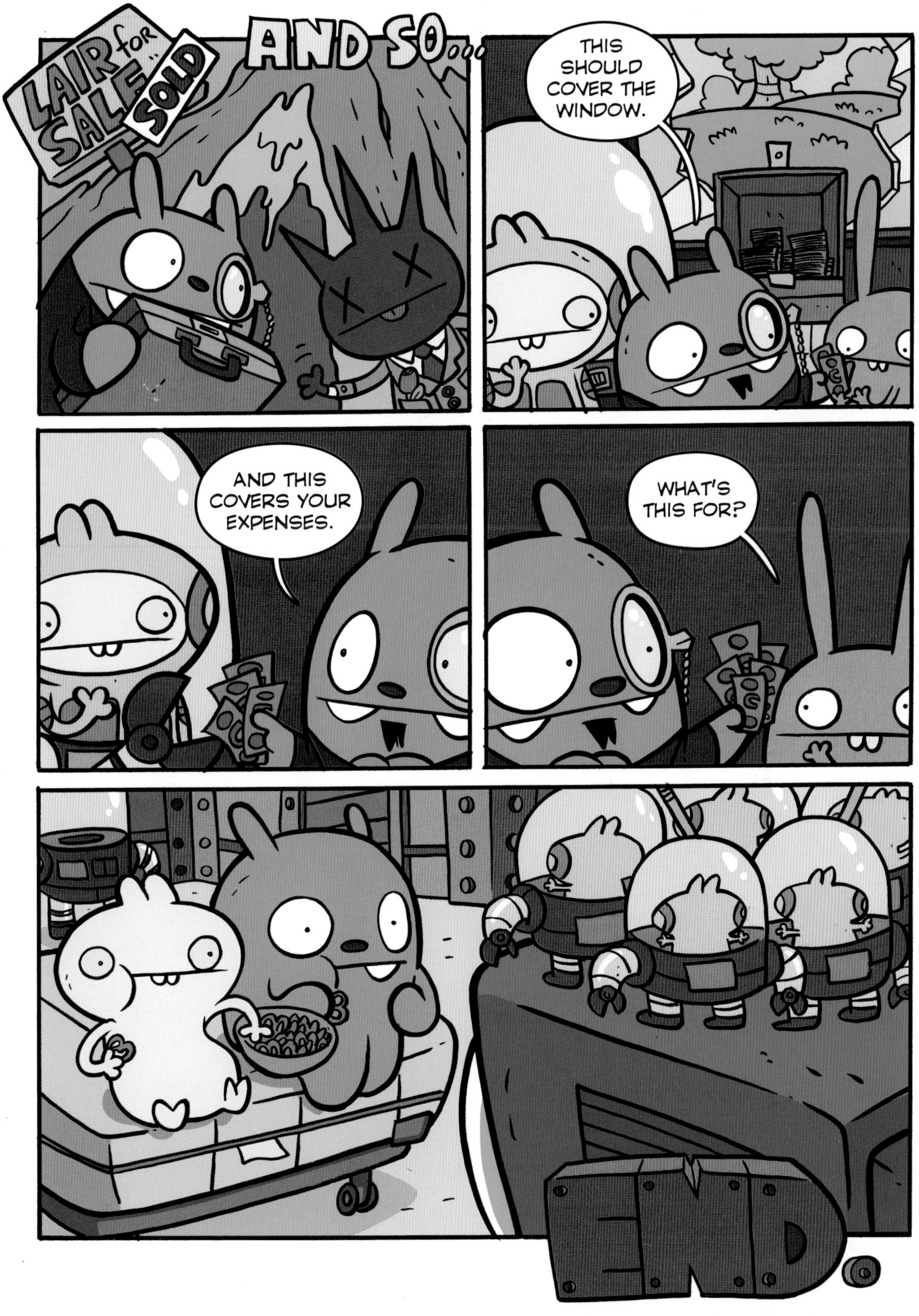
LAIR for SALE
SOLD
AND SO...
THIS SHOULD COVER THE WINDOW.
AND THIS COVERS YOUR EXPENSES.
WHAT'S THIS FOR?
END.

The Twelve

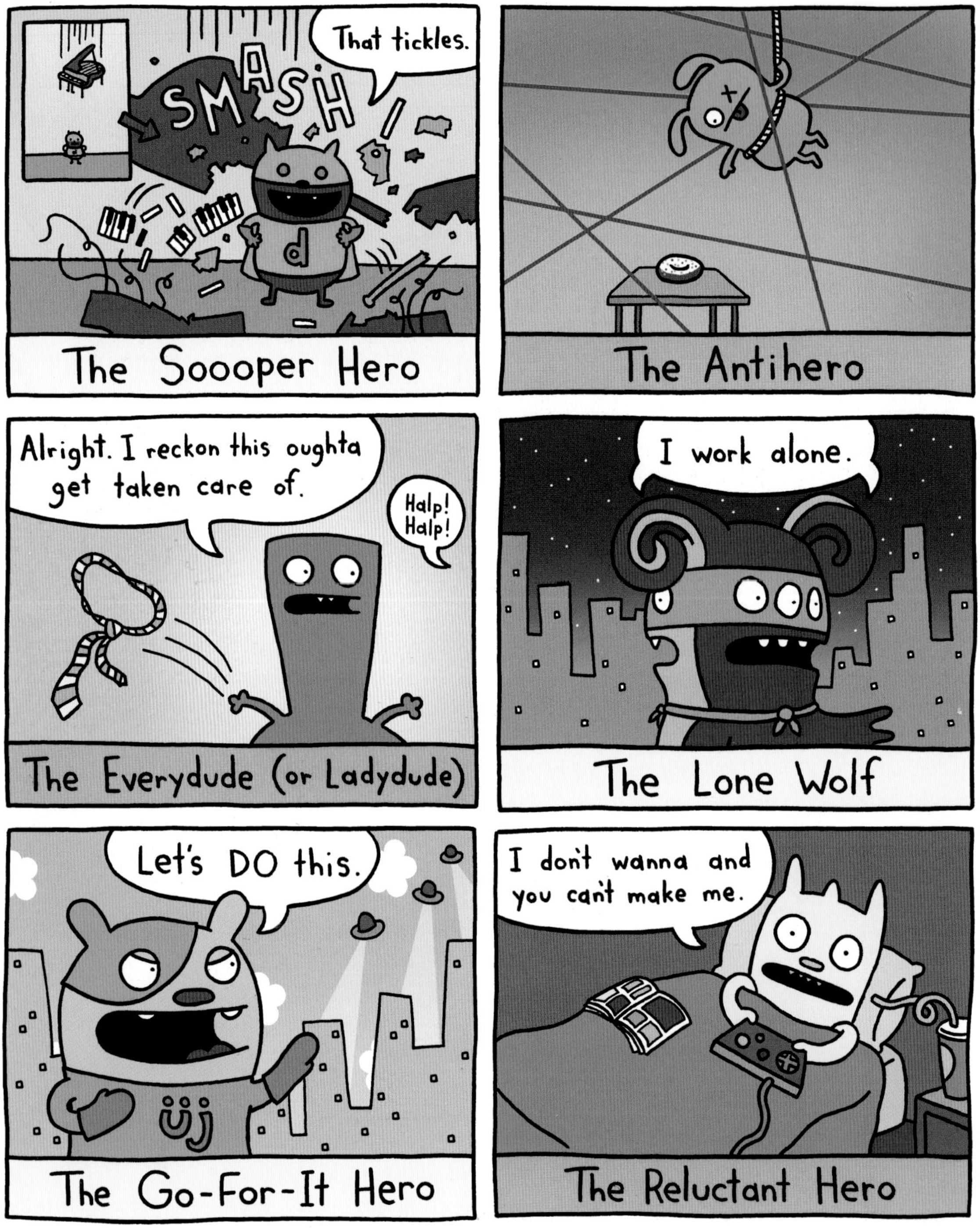
That tickles.
SMASH
The Soooper Hero
The Antihero
Alright. I reckon this oughta get taken care of.
Halp! Halp!
The Everydude (or Ladydude)
I work alone.
The Lone Wolf
Let's DO this.
The Go-For-It Hero
I don't wanna and you can't make me.
The Reluctant Hero

Heroic Types

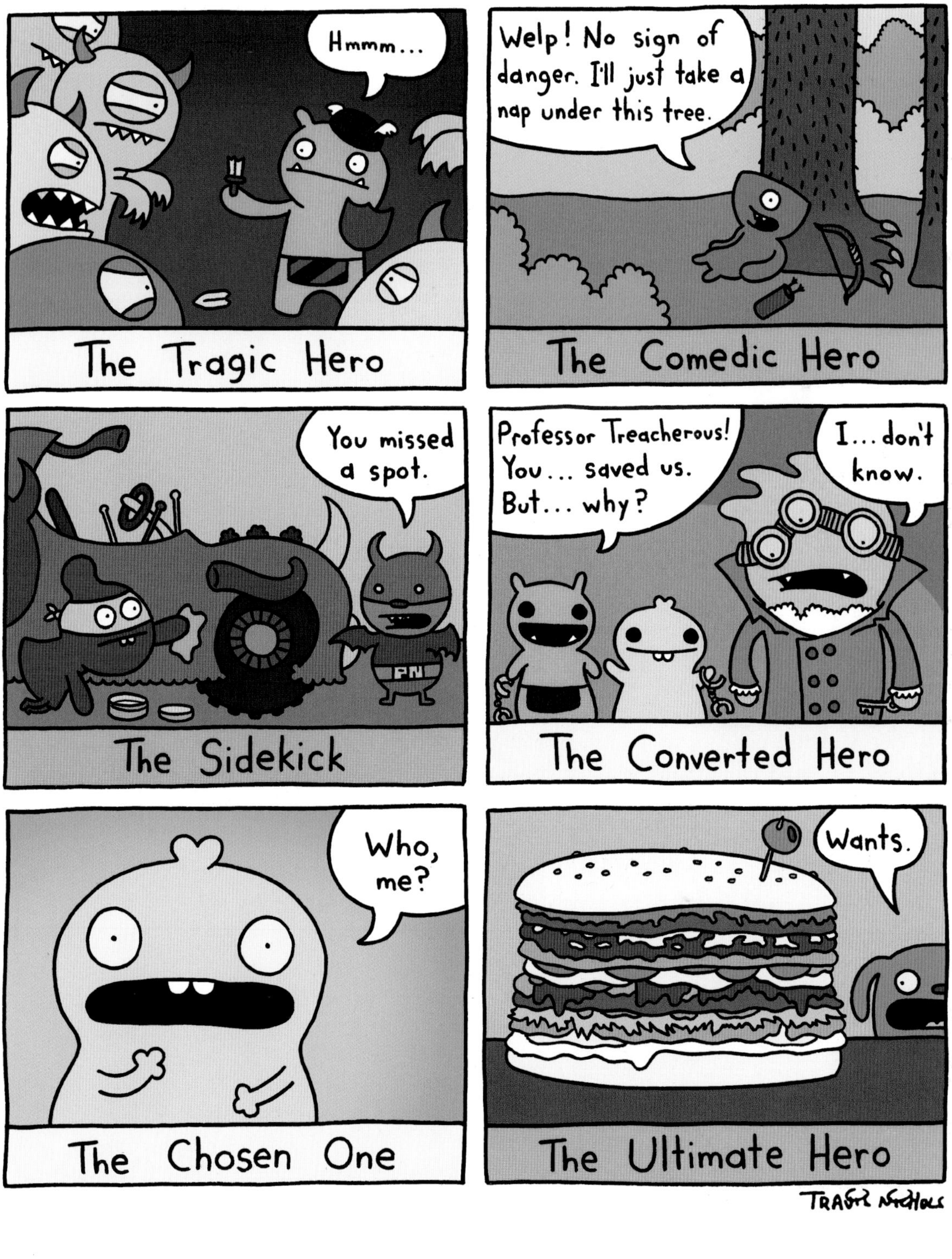
Hmmm...
The Tragic Hero
Welp! No sign of danger. I'll just take a nap under this tree.
The Comedic Hero
You missed a spot.
PN
The Sidekick
Professor Treacherous! You... saved us. But... why?
I... don't know.
The Converted Hero
Who, me?
The Chosen One
Wants.
The Ultimate Hero
TRAVIS NICHOLS

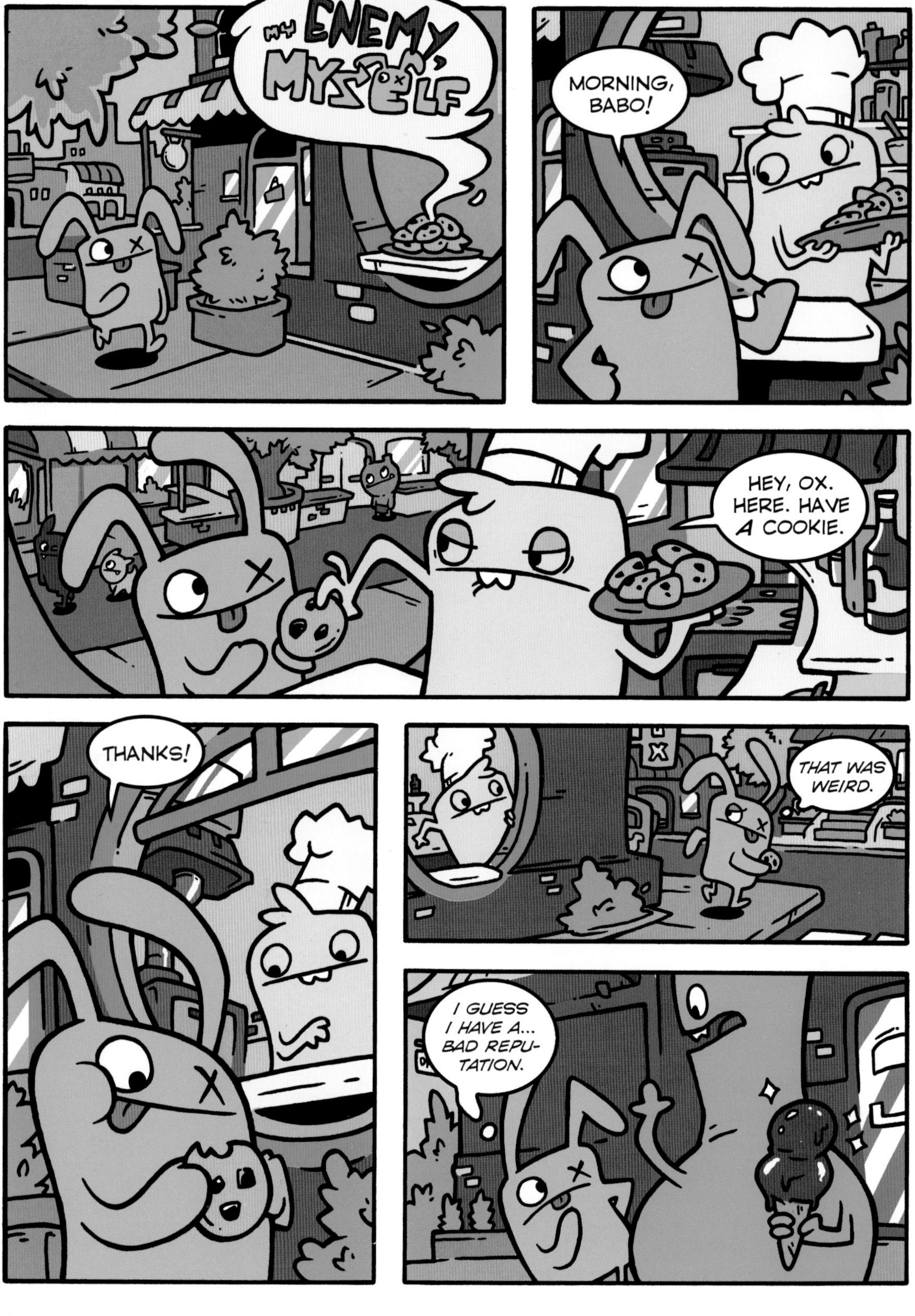
MY ENEMY, MYSELF
MORNING, BABO!
HEY, OX. HERE. HAVE A COOKIE.
THANKS!
THAT WAS WEIRD.
I GUESS I HAVE A... BAD REPUTATION.

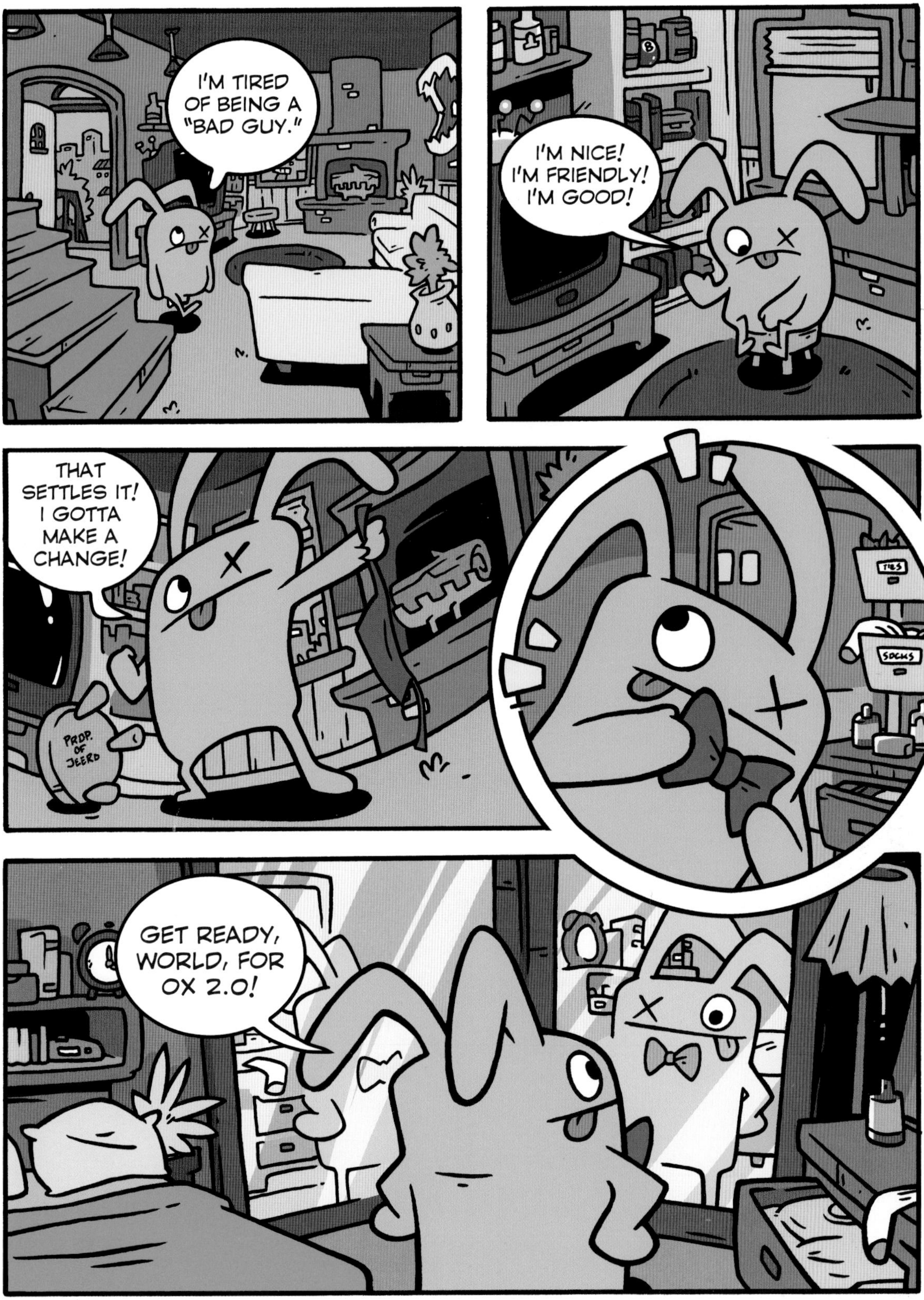

I'M TIRED OF BEING A "BAD GUY."
I'M NICE! I'M FRIENDLY! I'M GOOD!
THAT SETTLES IT! I GOTTA MAKE A CHANGE!
PROP. OF JEERD
TIES
SOCKS
GET READY, WORLD, FOR OX 2.0!

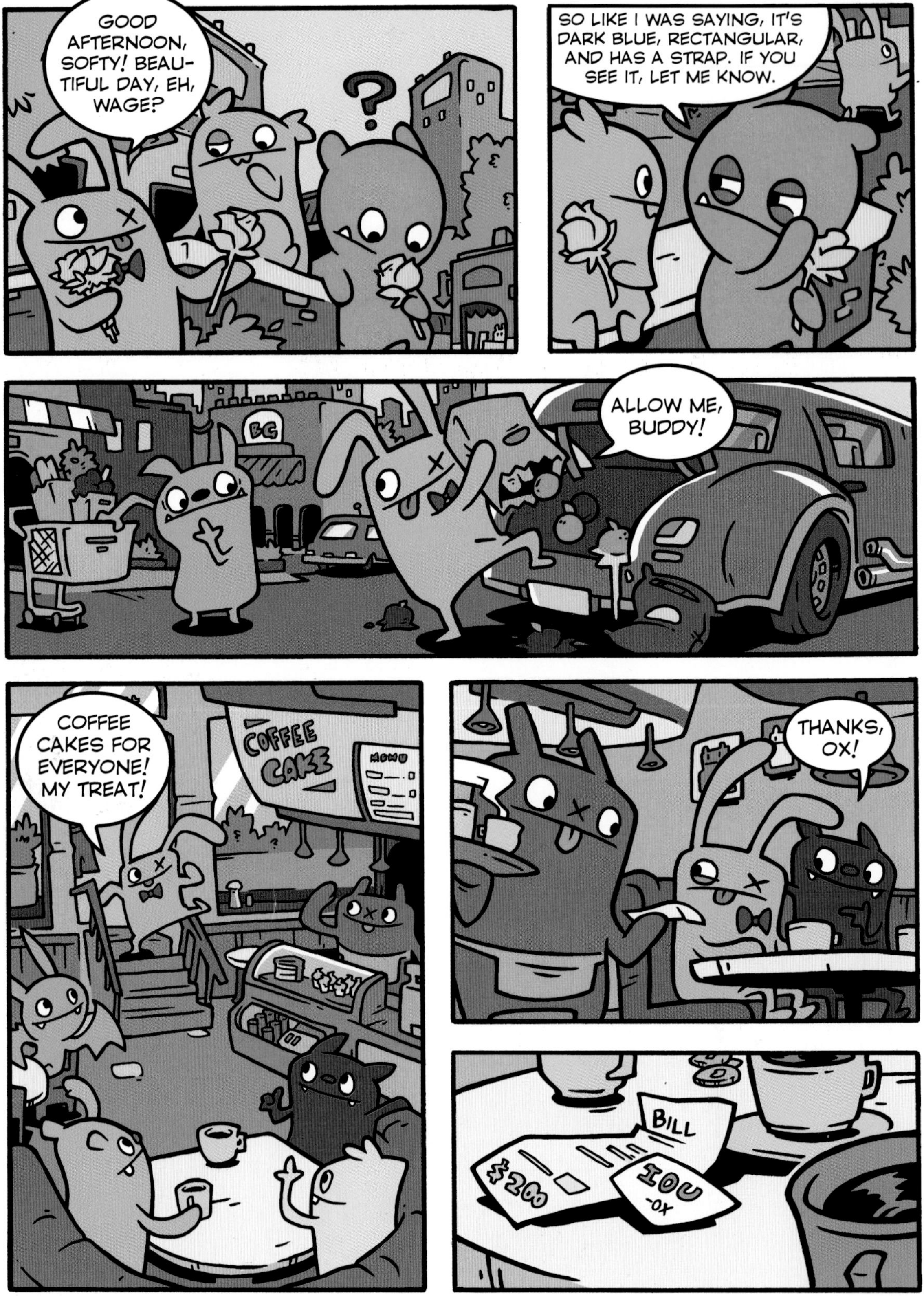
GOOD AFTERNOON, SOFTY! BEAU-TIFUL DAY, EH, WAGE?
?
SO LIKE I WAS SAYING, IT'S DARK BLUE, RECTANGULAR, AND HAS A STRAP. IF YOU SEE IT, LET ME KNOW.
BG
ALLOW ME, BUDDY!
COFFEE CAKES FOR EVERYONE! MY TREAT!
COFFEE CAKE
MENU
THANKS, OX!
BILL
$200
IOU -OX

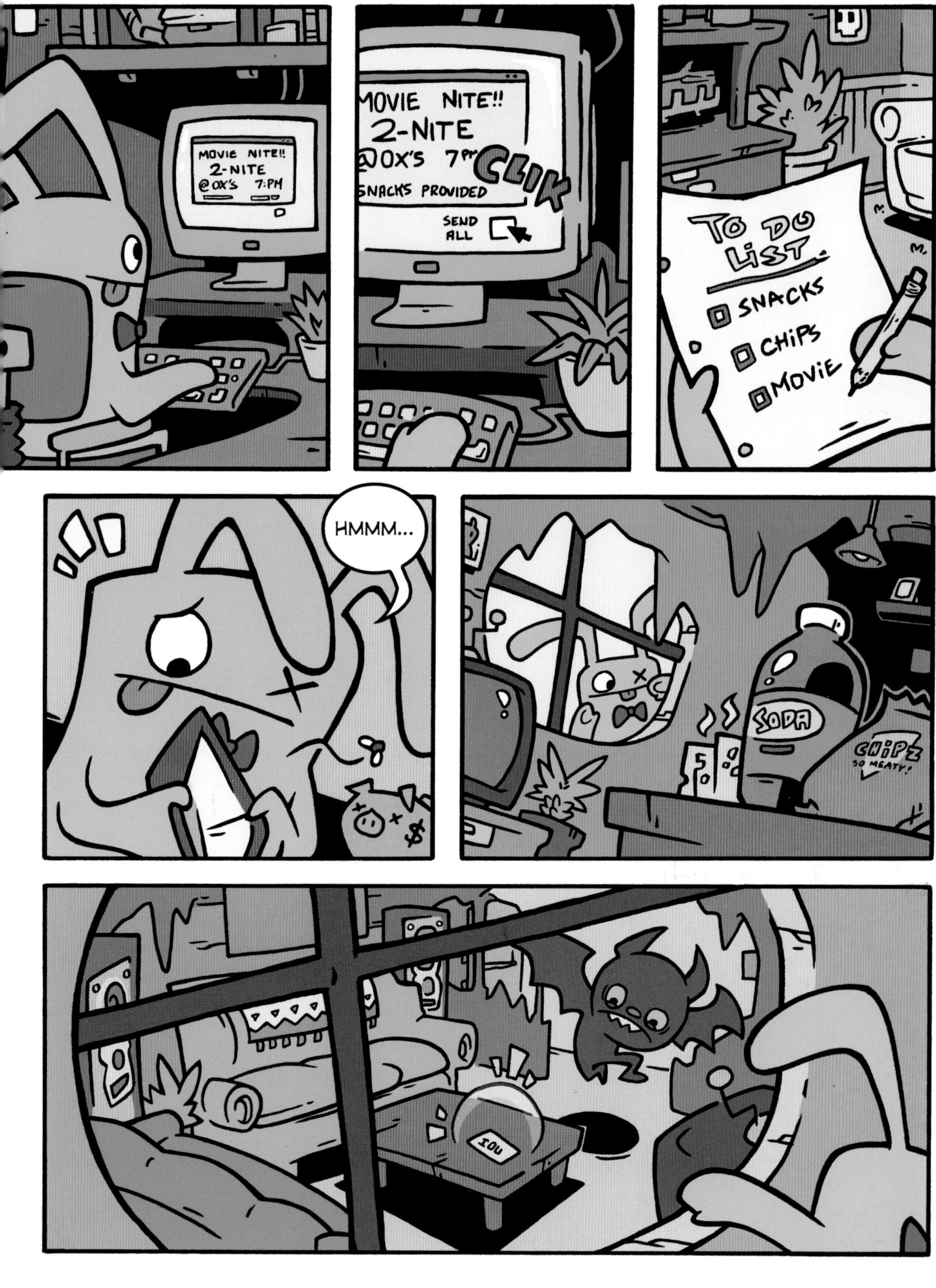
MOVIE NITE!!
2-NITE
@OX'S 7:PM
MOVIE NITE!!
2-NITE
@OX'S 7PM
SNACKS PROVIDED
SEND ALL
CLIK
TO DO LIST
SNACKS
CHIPS
MOVIE
HMMM...
SODA
CHIPZ
SO MEATY!
IOU

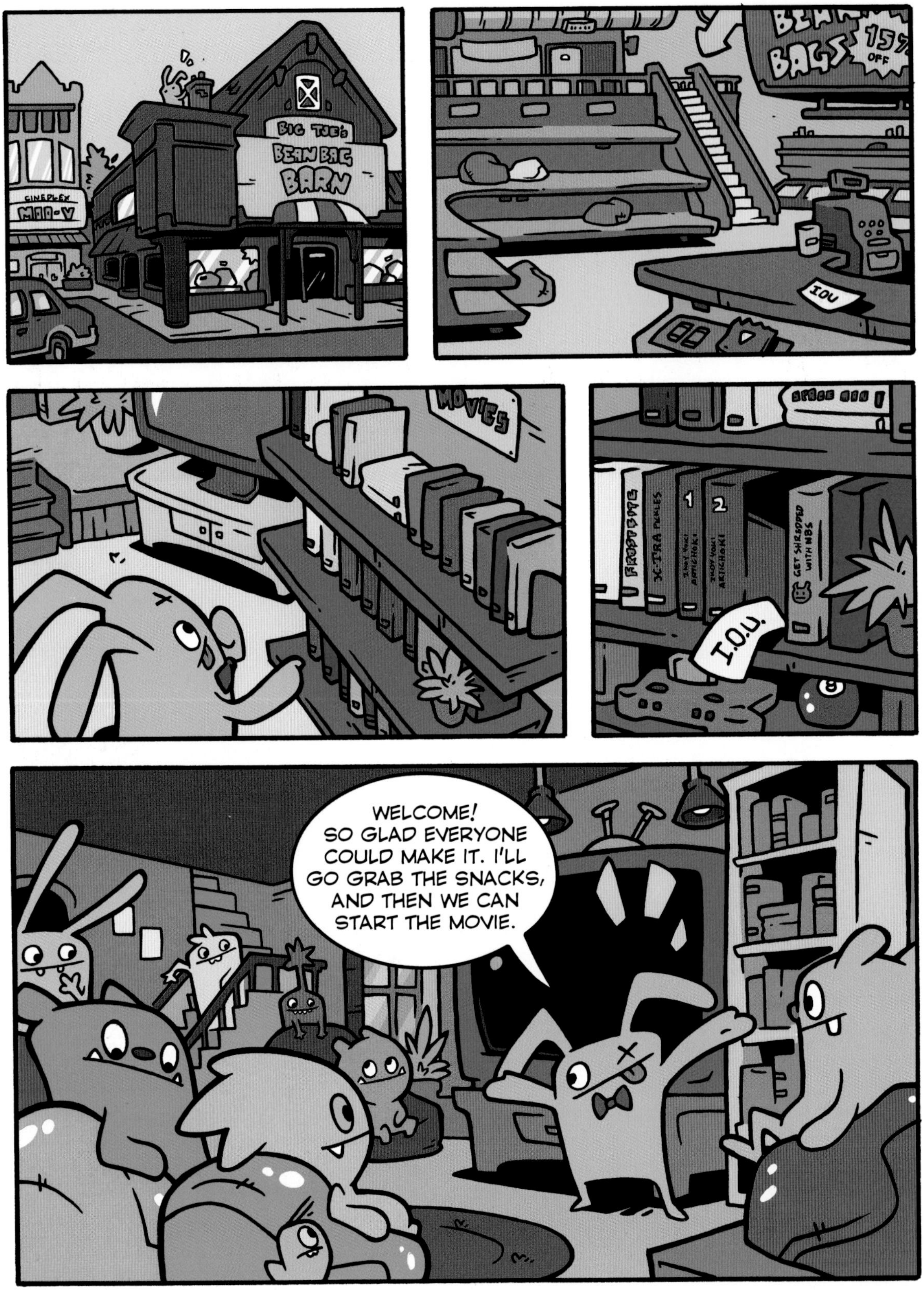
BIG TOE'S
BEAN BAG
BARN
CINEPLEX
IOU
MOVIES
I.O.U.
WELCOME! SO GLAD EVERYONE COULD MAKE IT. I'LL GO GRAB THE SNACKS, AND THEN WE CAN START THE MOVIE.

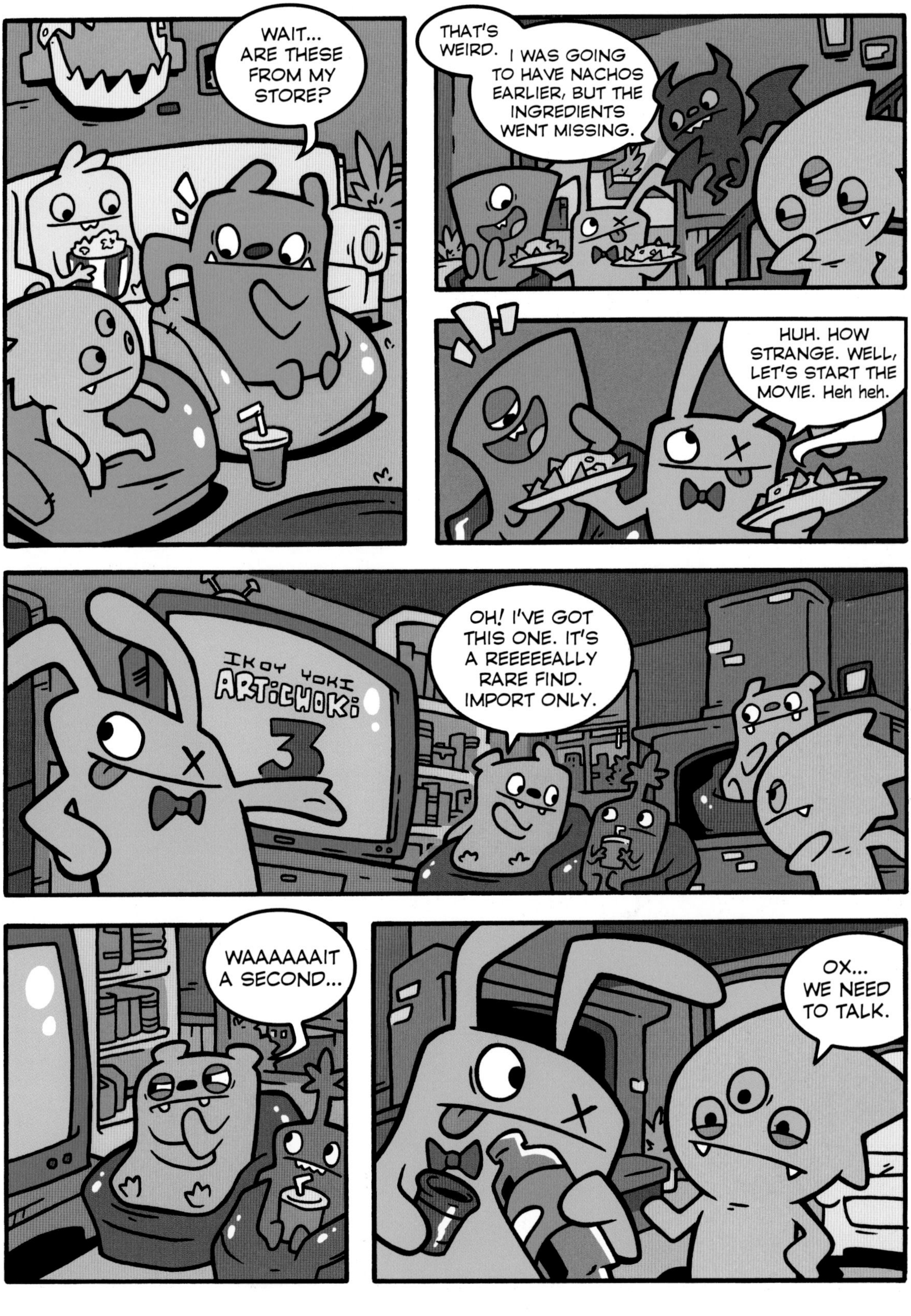
WAIT... ARE THESE FROM MY STORE?
THAT'S WEIRD.
I WAS GOING TO HAVE NACHOS EARLIER, BUT THE INGREDIENTS WENT MISSING.
HUH. HOW STRANGE. WELL, LET'S START THE MOVIE. Heh heh.
IKOY YOKI ARTICHOKI 3
OH! I'VE GOT THIS ONE. IT'S A REEEEEALLY RARE FIND. IMPORT ONLY.
WAAAAAAIT A SECOND...
OX... WE NEED TO TALK.

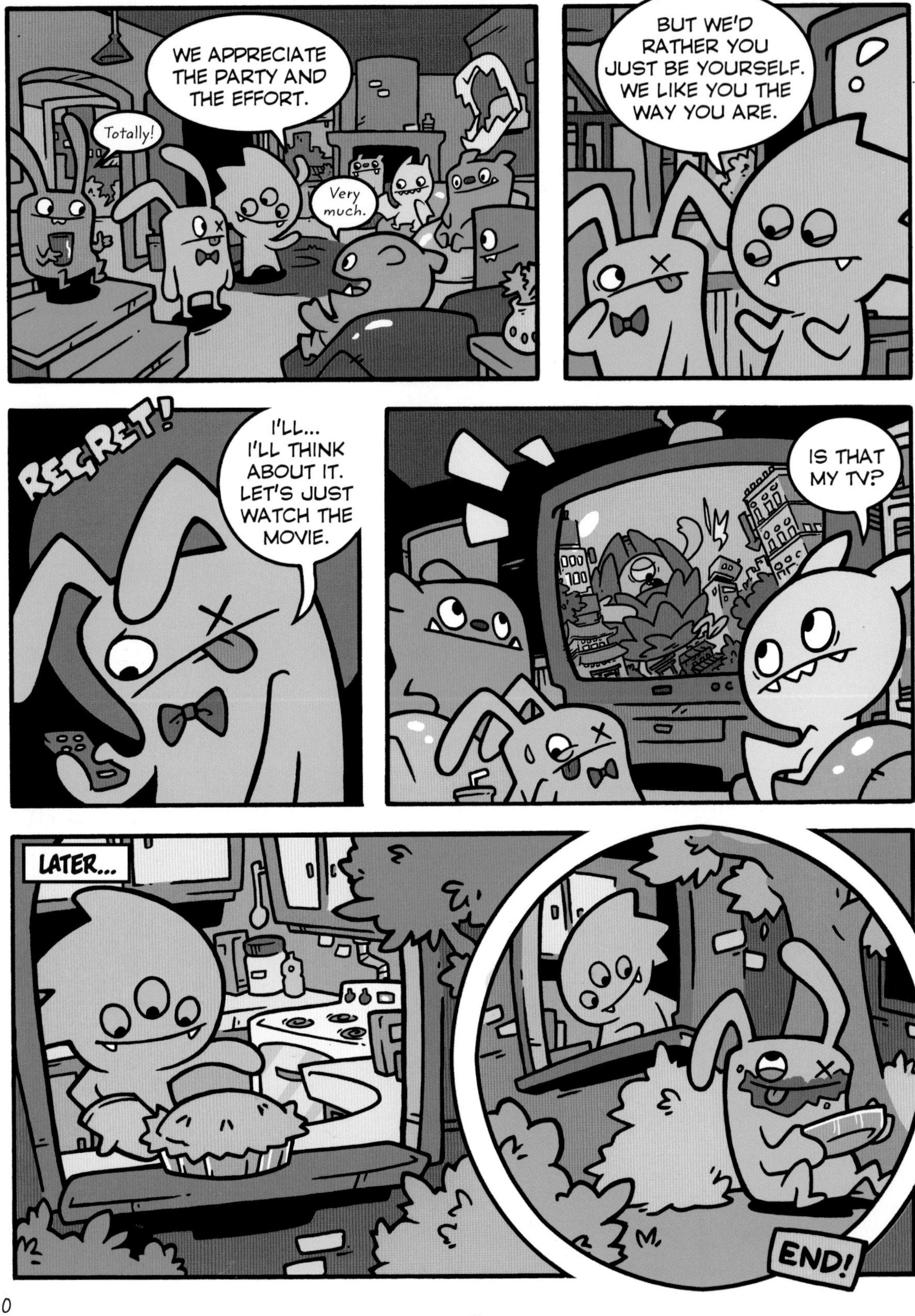
WE APPRECIATE THE PARTY AND THE EFFORT.
Totally!
Very much.
BUT WE'D RATHER YOU JUST BE YOURSELF. WE LIKE YOU THE WAY YOU ARE.
REGRET!
I'LL... I'LL THINK ABOUT IT. LET'S JUST WATCH THE MOVIE.
IS THAT MY TV?
LATER...
END!

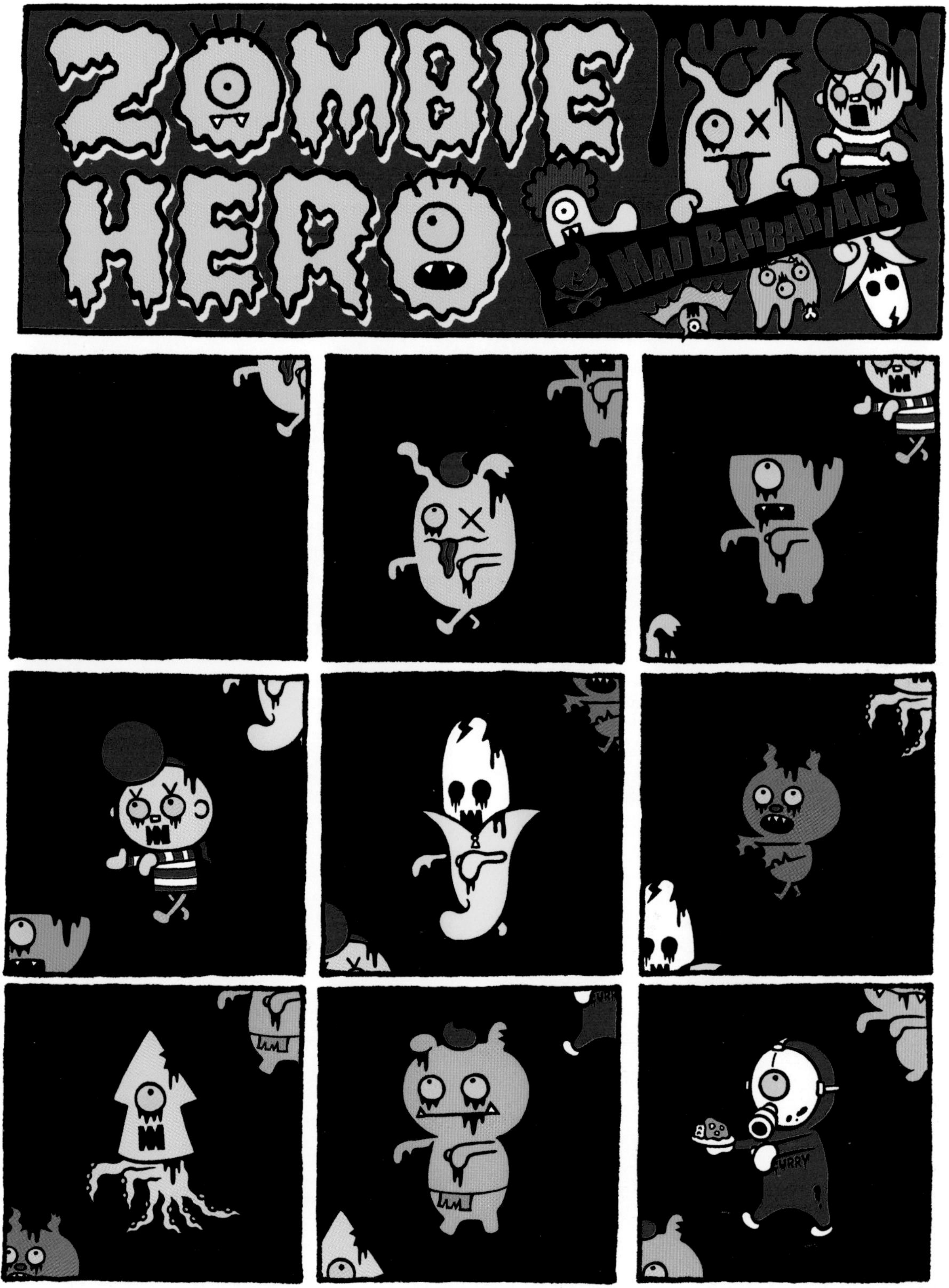
ZOMBIE HERO
MAD BARBARIANS
CURRY

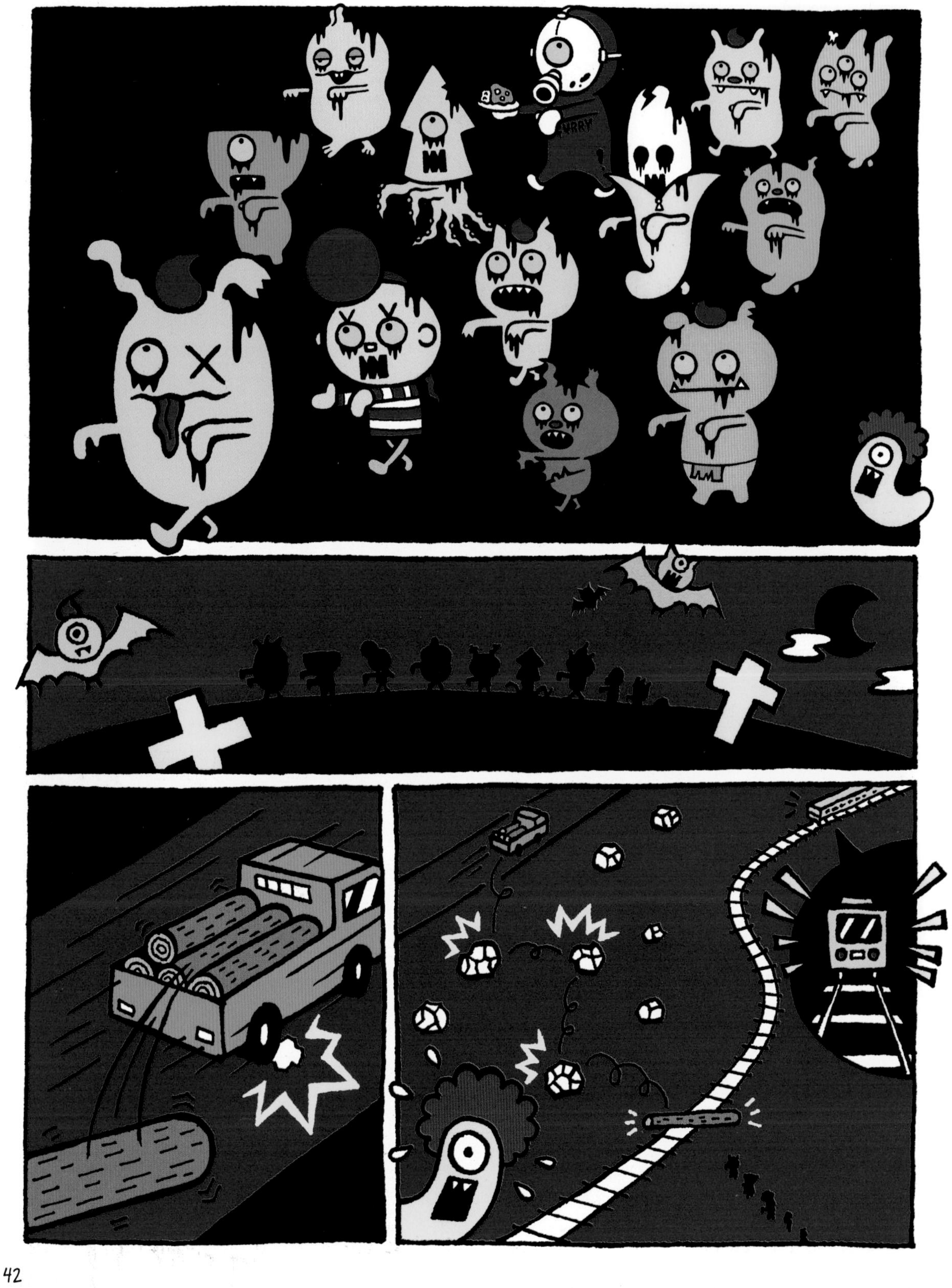

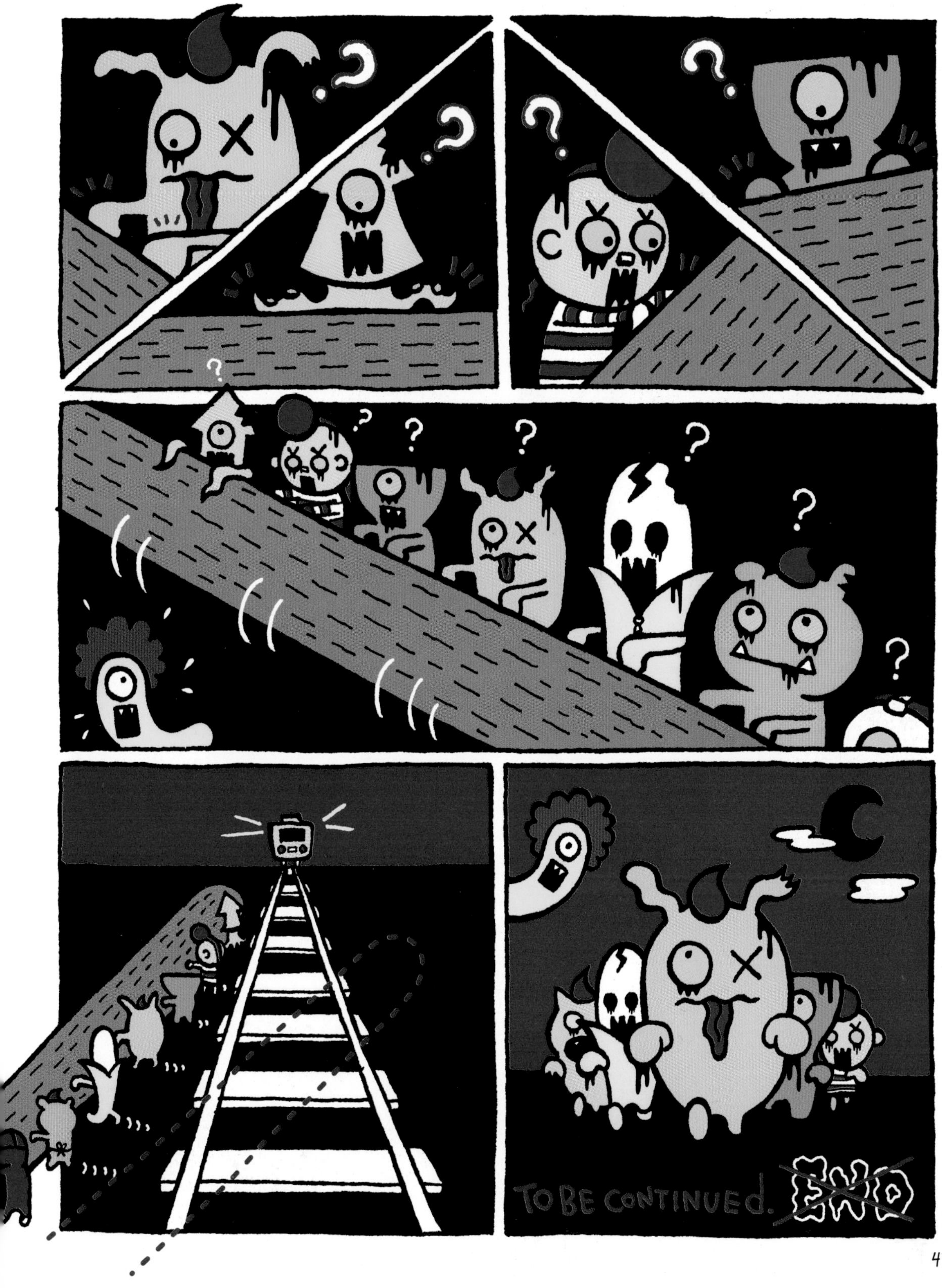
TO BE CONTINUED.
END

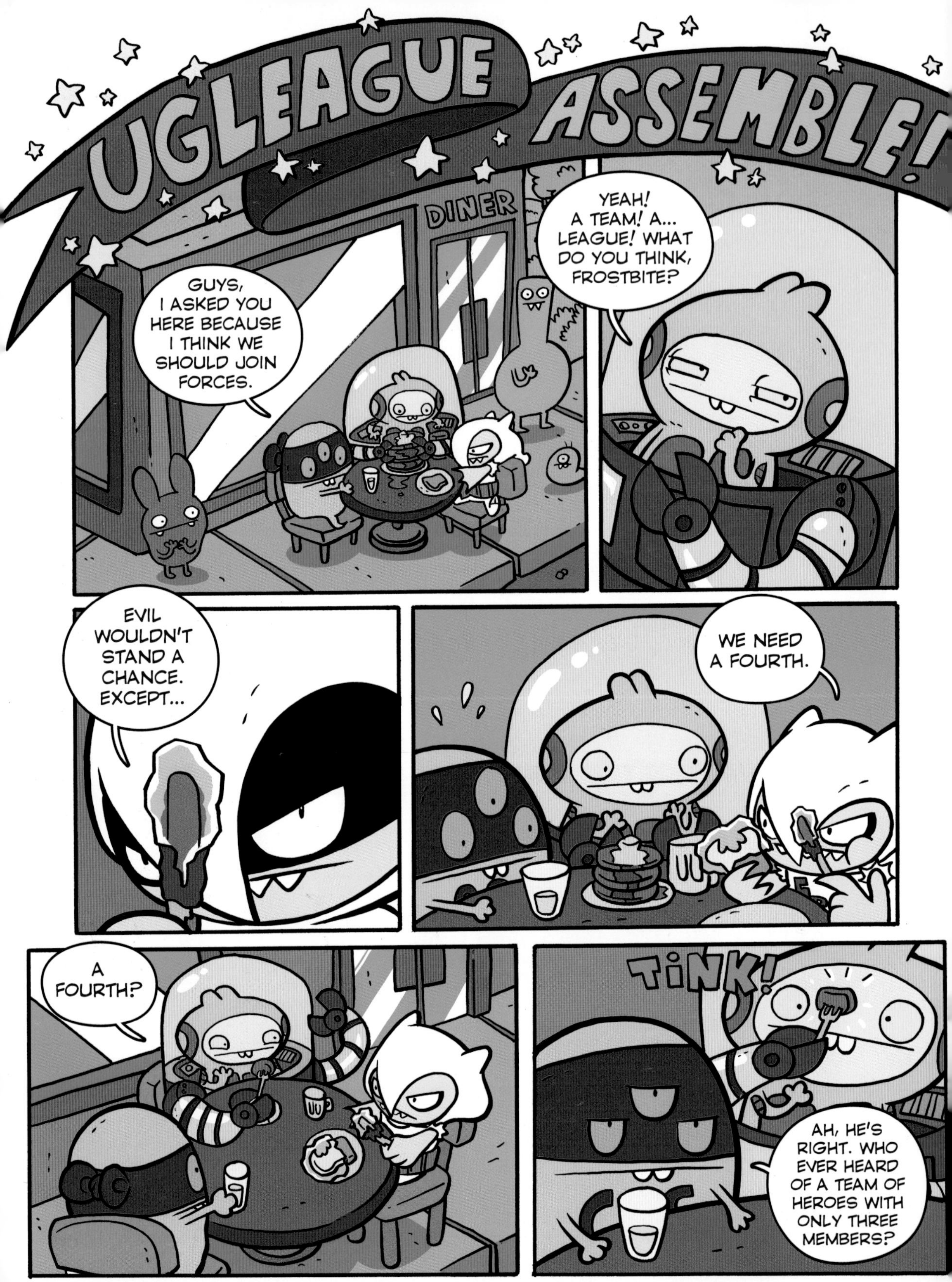
UGLEAGUE ASSEMBLE!
DINER
GUYS, I ASKED YOU HERE BECAUSE I THINK WE SHOULD JOIN FORCES.
YEAH! A TEAM! A... LEAGUE! WHAT DO YOU THINK, FROSTBITE?
EVIL WOULDN'T STAND A CHANCE. EXCEPT...
WE NEED A FOURTH.
A FOURTH?
TINK!
AH, HE'S RIGHT. WHO EVER HEARD OF A TEAM OF HEROES WITH ONLY THREE MEMBERS?

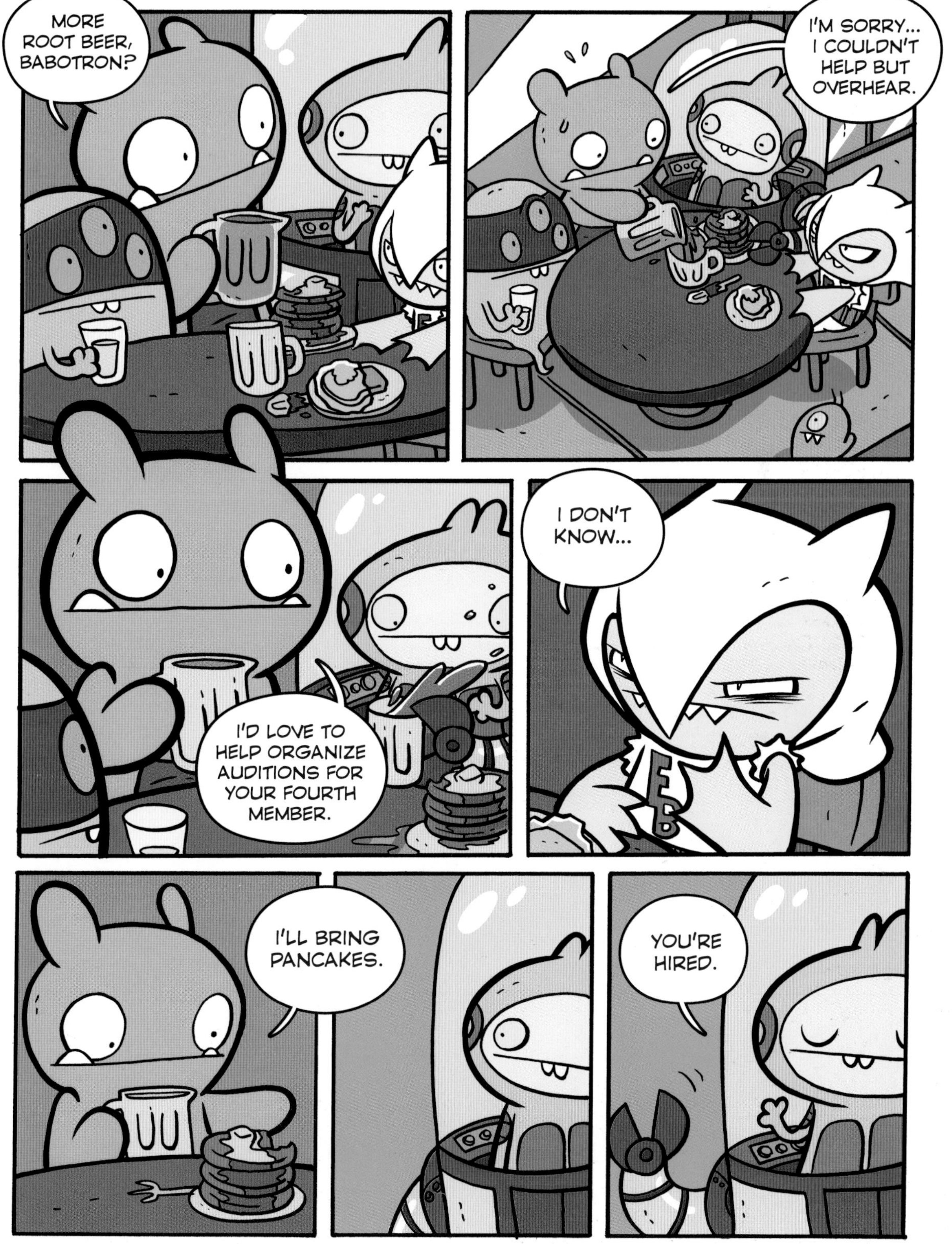
MORE ROOT BEER, BABOTRON?
I'M SORRY... I COULDN'T HELP BUT OVERHEAR.
I'D LOVE TO HELP ORGANIZE AUDITIONS FOR YOUR FOURTH MEMBER.
I DON'T KNOW...
I'LL BRING PANCAKES.
YOU'RE HIRED.

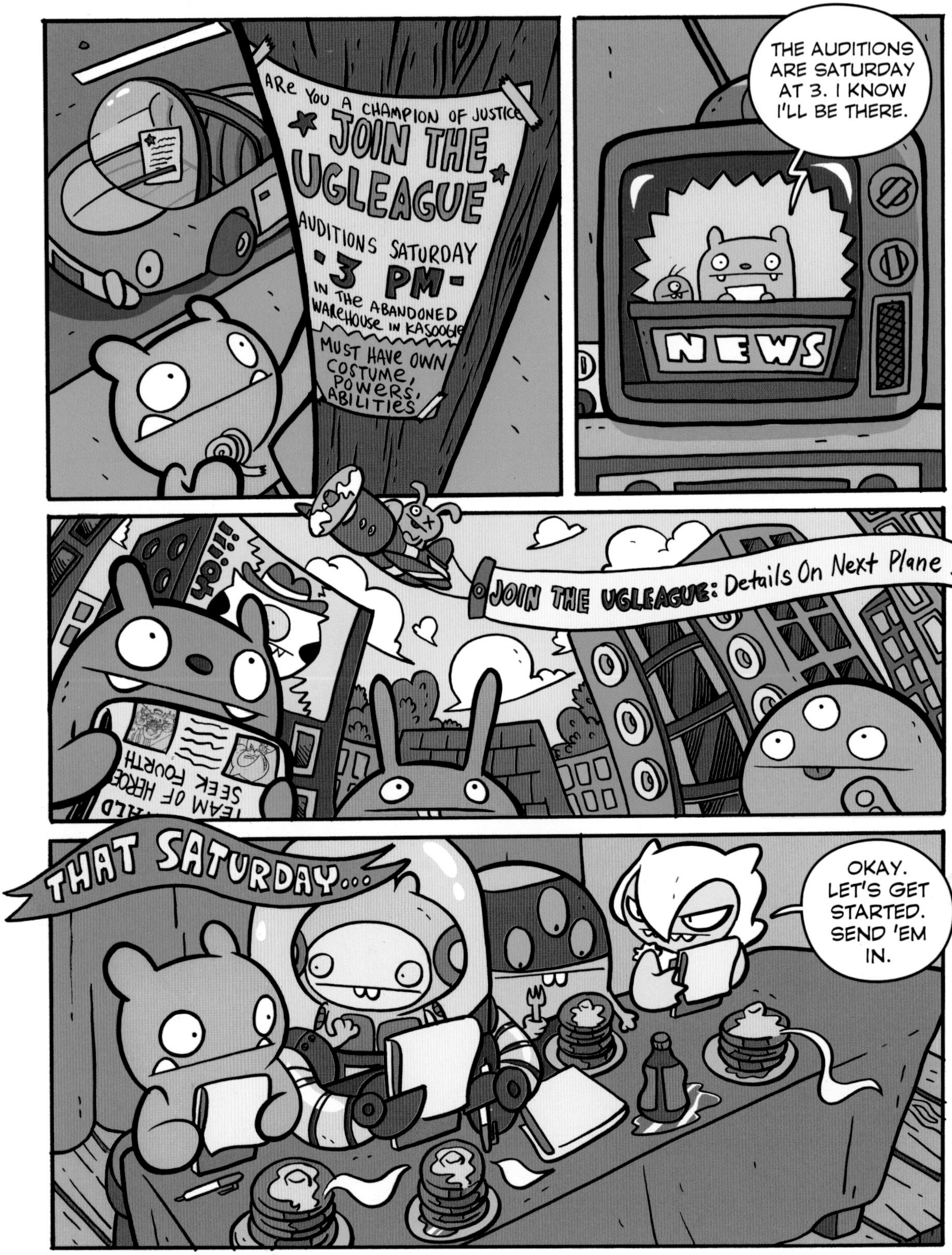
ARE YOU A CHAMPION OF JUSTICE
JOIN THE UGLEAGUE
AUDITIONS SATURDAY
-3 PM-
IN THE ABANDONED WAREHOUSE IN KASOOGIE
MUST HAVE OWN COSTUME, POWERS, ABILITIES
THE AUDITIONS ARE SATURDAY AT 3. I KNOW I'LL BE THERE.
NEWS
JOIN THE UGLEAGUE: Details On Next Plane !!!
THAT SATURDAY...
OKAY. LET'S GET STARTED. SEND 'EM IN.

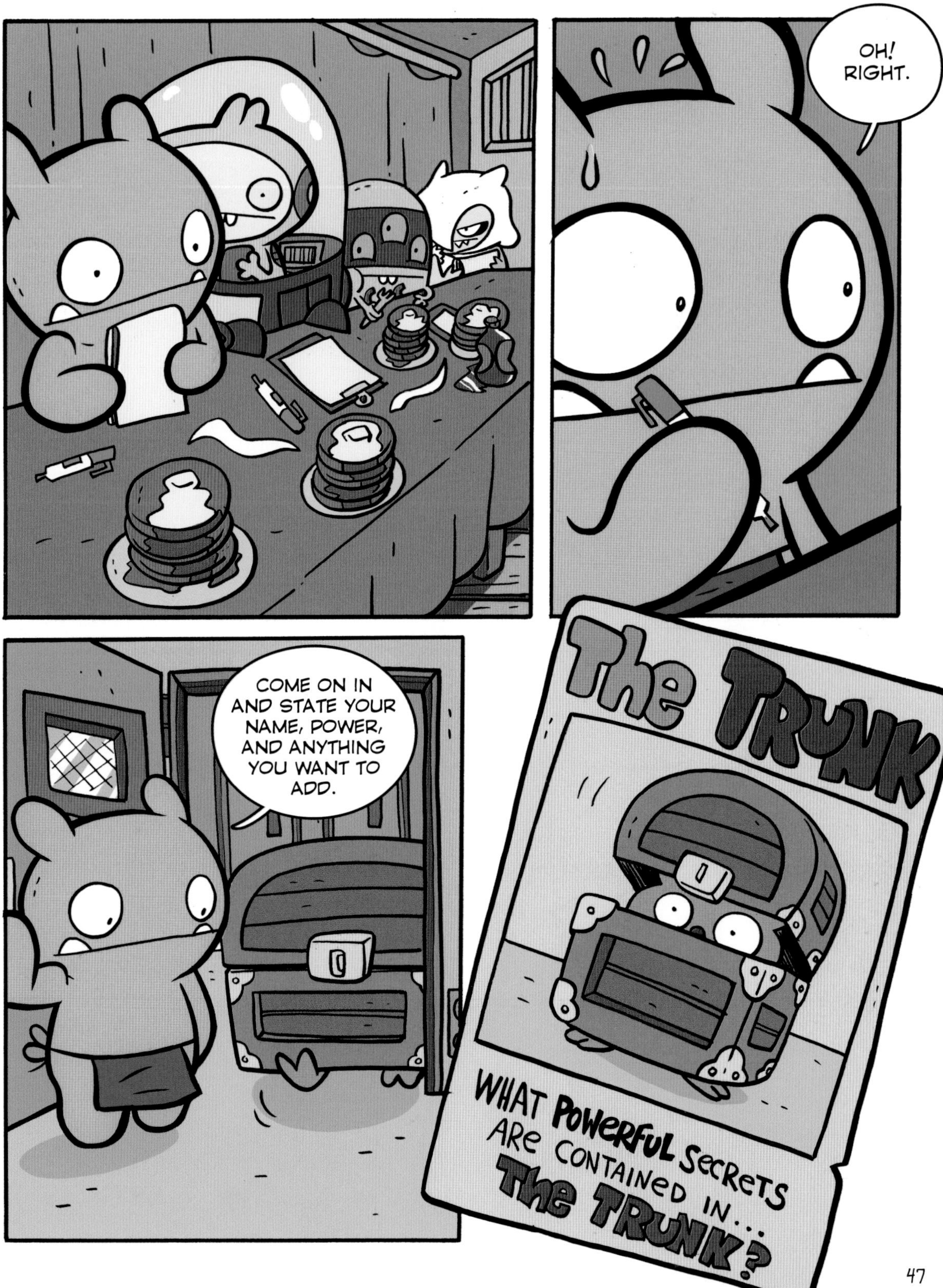
OH! RIGHT.
COME ON IN AND STATE YOUR NAME, POWER, AND ANYTHING YOU WANT TO ADD.
The TRUNK
WHAT POWERFUL SECRETS ARE CONTAINED IN... The TRUNK?

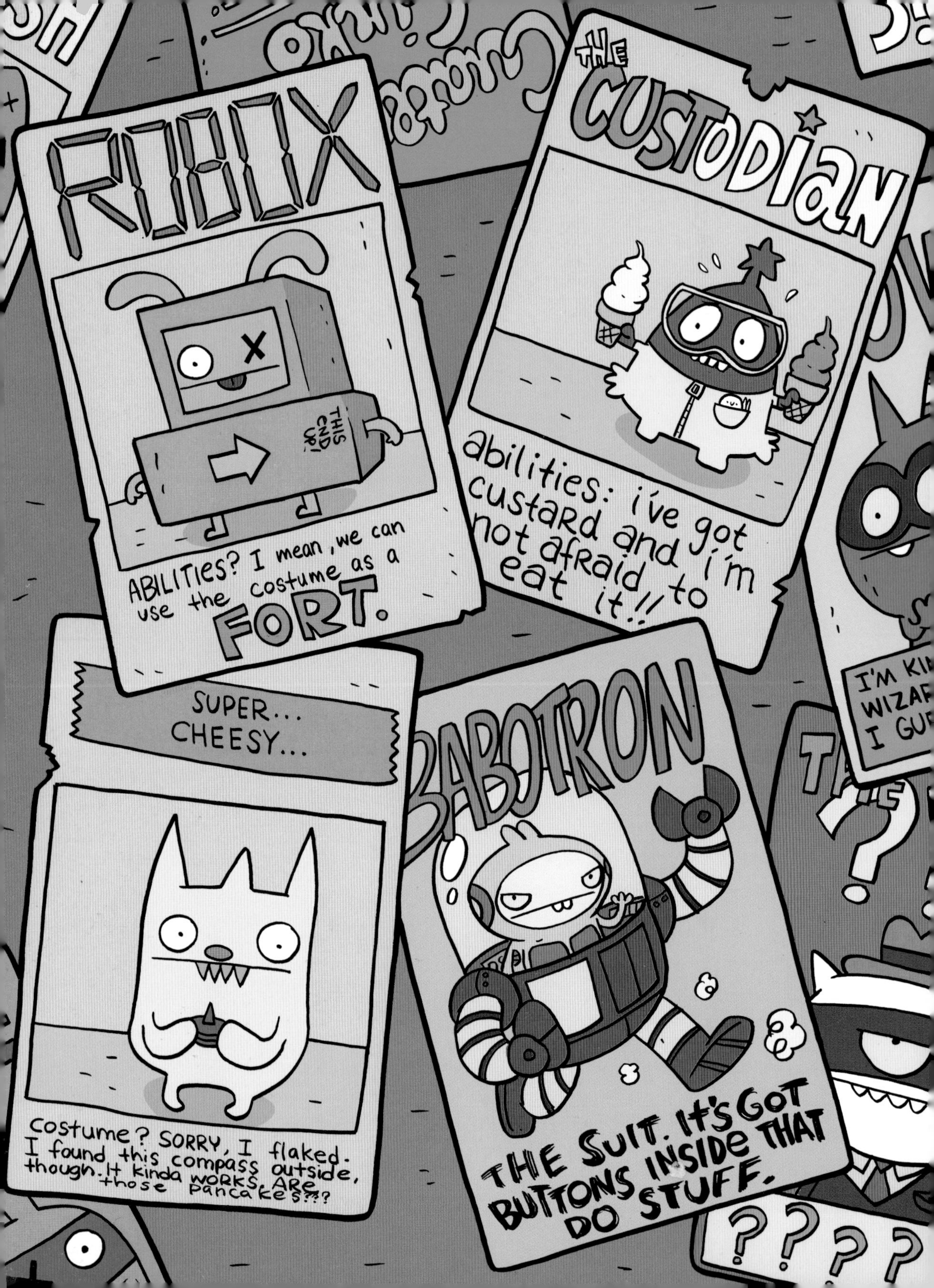

ROBOX
THIS END UP!
ABILITIES? I mean, we can use the costume as a FORT.
THE CUSTODIAN
abilities: i've got custard and i'm not afraid to eat it!!
SUPER... CHEESY...
costume? SORRY, I flaked. I found this compass outside, though. It kinda WORKS. ARE those pancakes???
BABOTRON
THE SUIT. IT'S GOT BUTTONS INSIDE THAT DO STUFF.
I'M KI
WIZAR
I GU
???

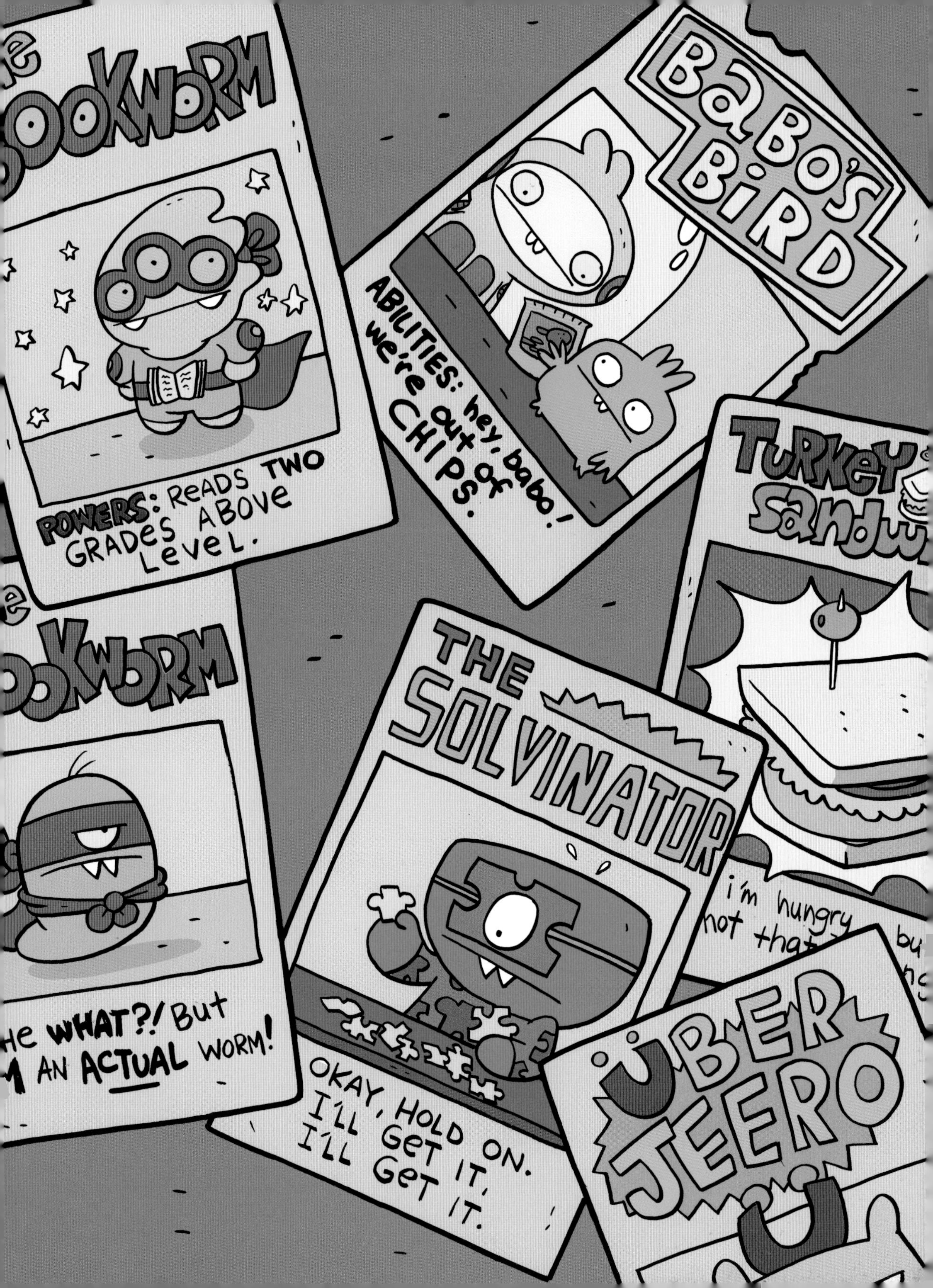

BOOKWORM
POWERS: READS TWO GRADES ABOVE LEVEL.
BABO'S BIRD
ABILITIES: hey, babo! we're out of CHIPS.
TURKEY Sandw
i'm hungry
not that
BOOKWORM
THE WHAT?! But
AN ACTUAL WORM!
THE SOLVINATOR
OKAY, HOLD ON. I'LL GET IT. I'LL GET IT.
UBER JEERO

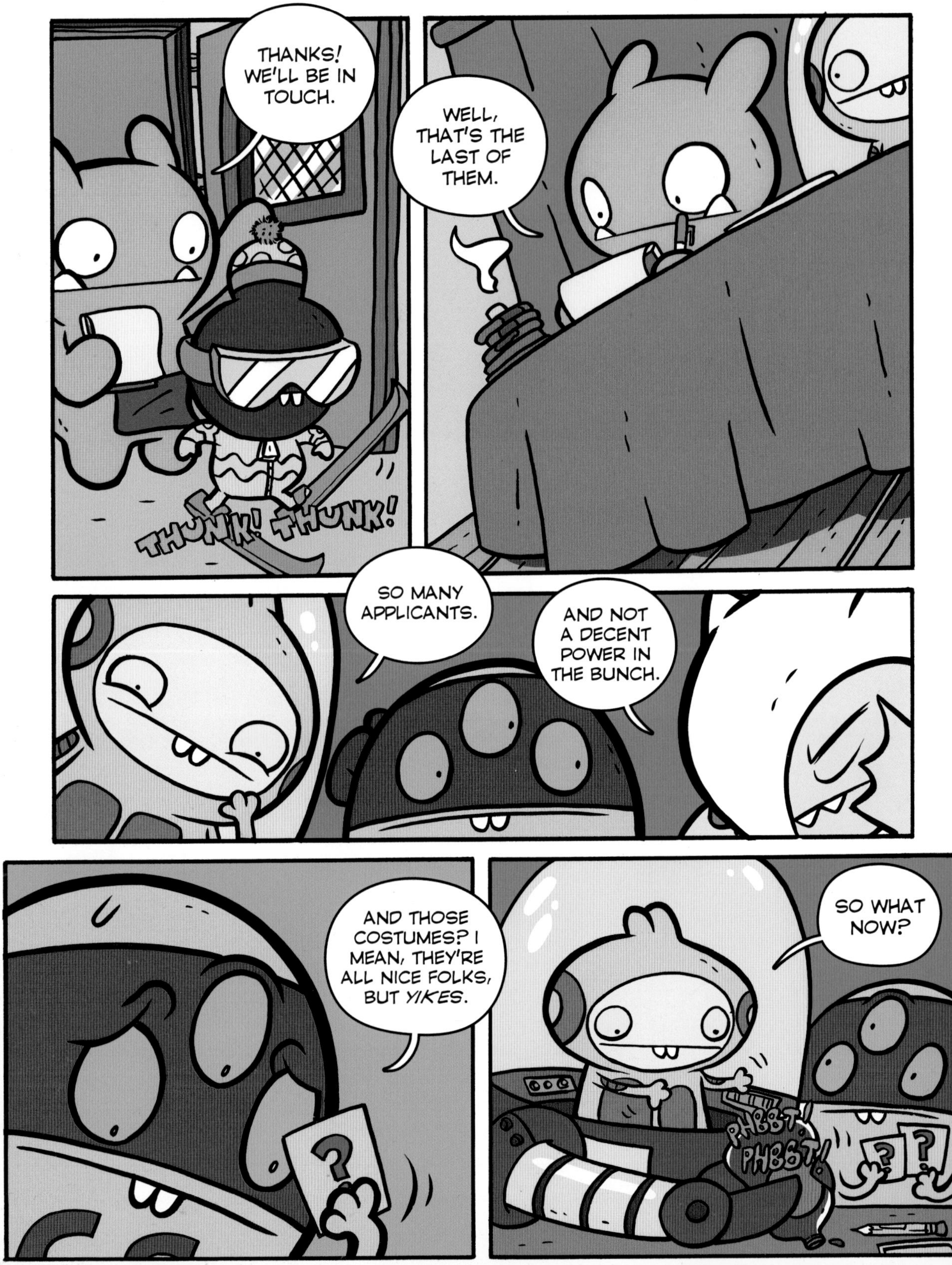
THANKS! WE'LL BE IN TOUCH.
THUNK! THUNK!
WELL, THAT'S THE LAST OF THEM.
SO MANY APPLICANTS.
AND NOT A DECENT POWER IN THE BUNCH.
AND THOSE COSTUMES? I MEAN, THEY'RE ALL NICE FOLKS, BUT *YIKES*.
SO WHAT NOW?
PHBBT! PHBBT!

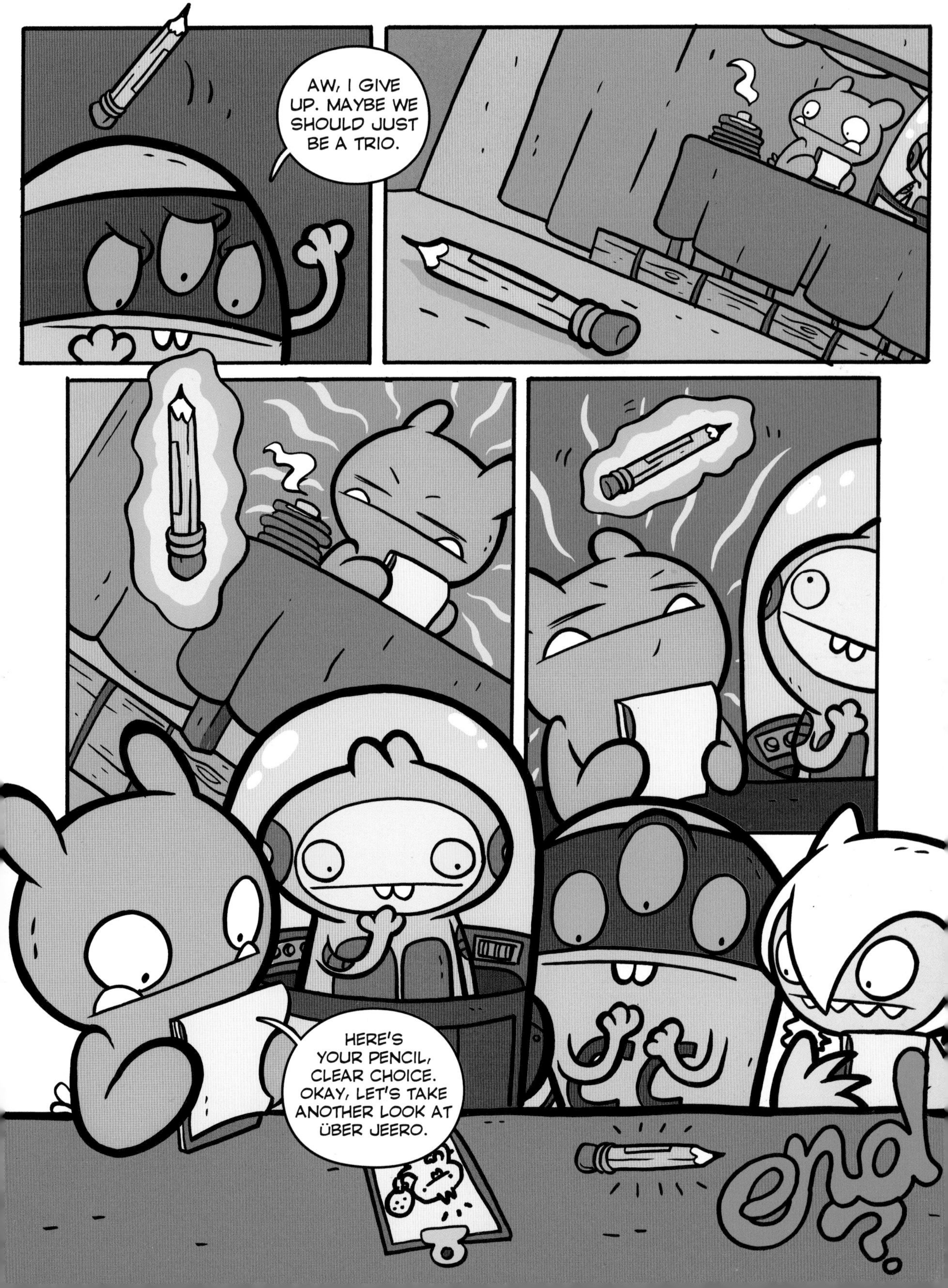
AW, I GIVE UP. MAYBE WE SHOULD JUST BE A TRIO.
HERE'S YOUR PENCIL, CLEAR CHOICE. OKAY, LET'S TAKE ANOTHER LOOK AT ÜBER JEERO.
end?

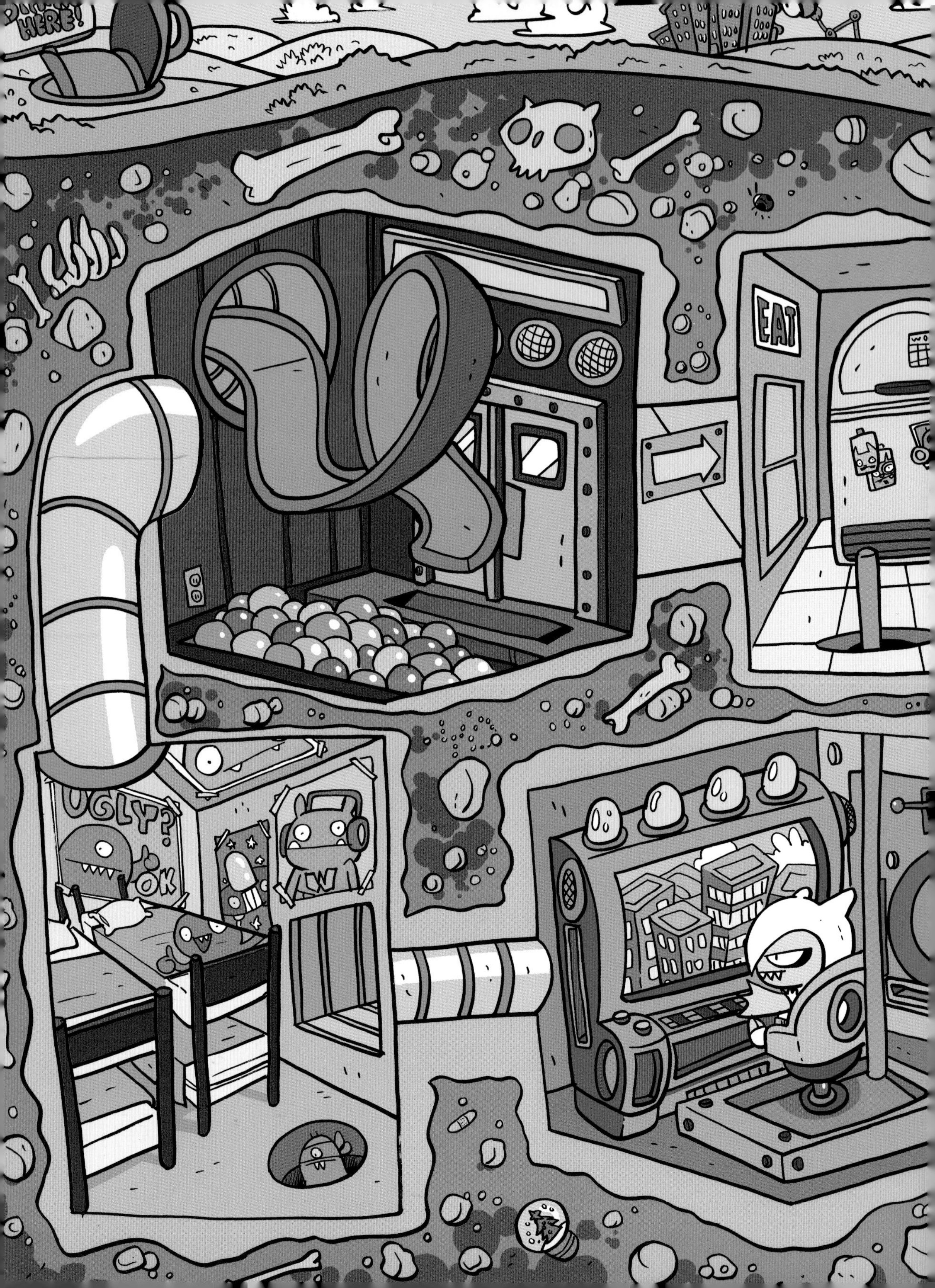
HERE!
EAT
UGLY?
OK

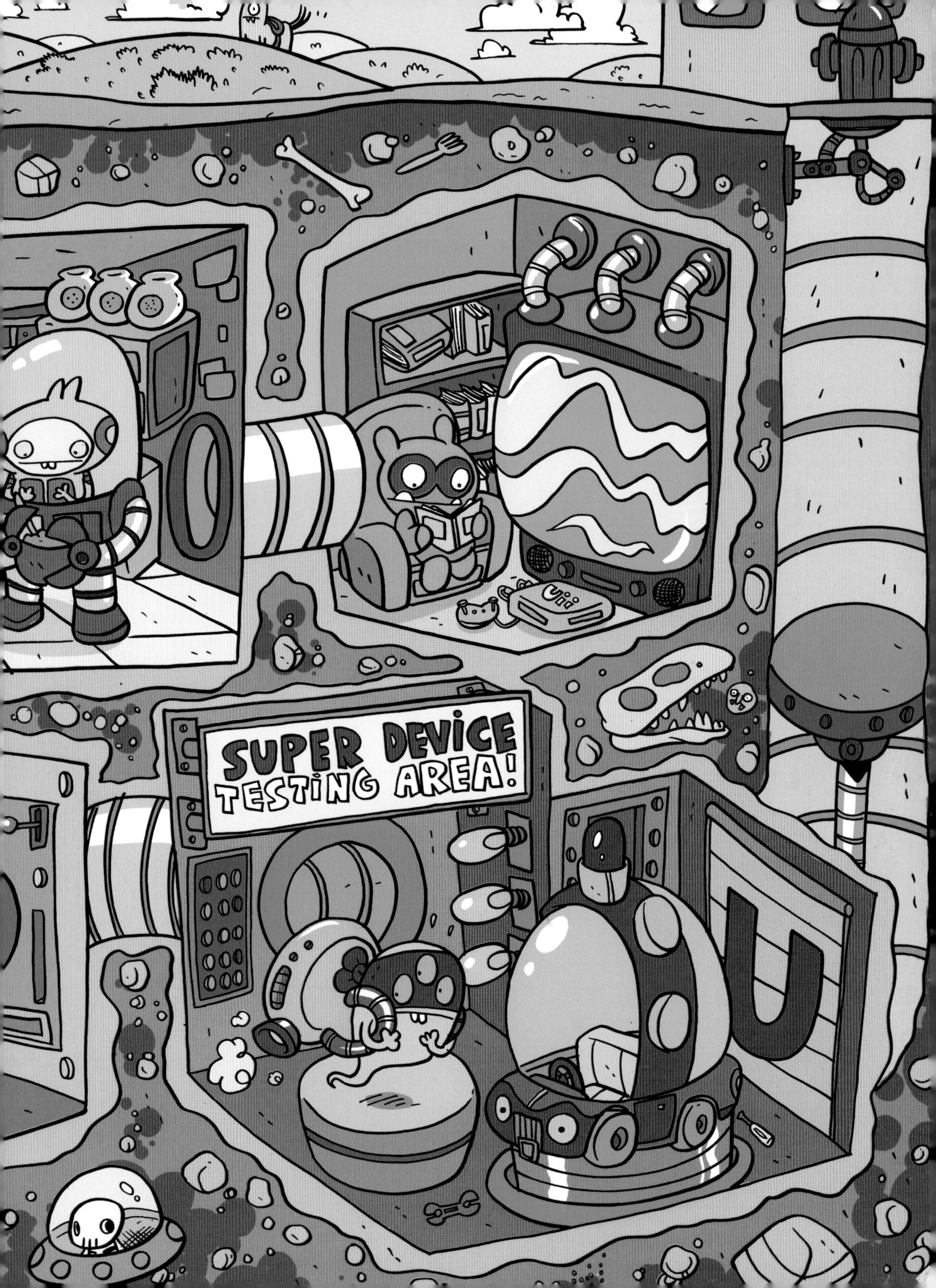
SUPER DEVICE
TESTING AREA!

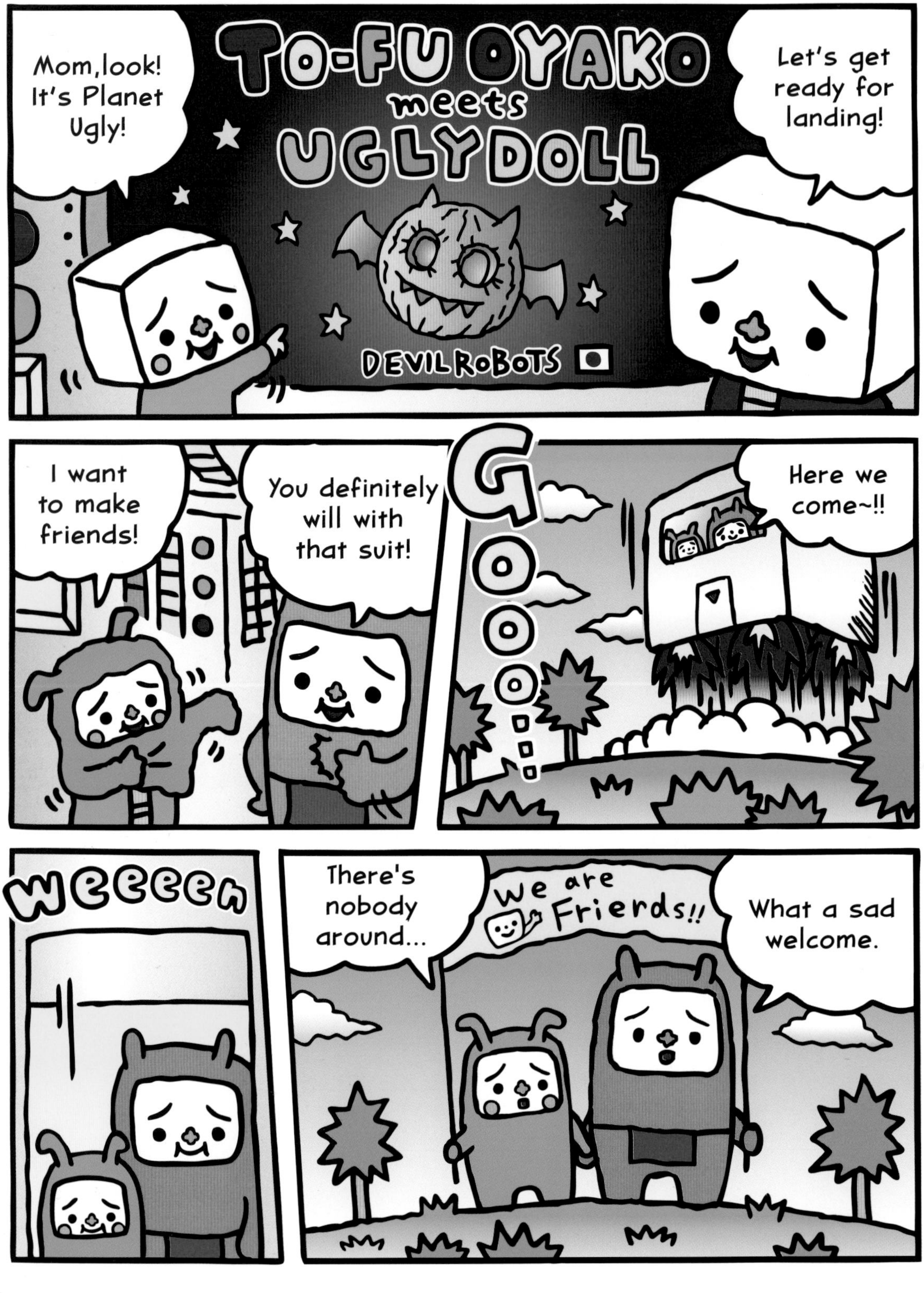
TO-FU OYAKO meets UGLYDOLL
DEVILROBOTS
Mom,look! It's Planet Ugly!
Let's get ready for landing!
I want to make friends!
You definitely will with that suit!
GOOOO...!!!
Here we come~!!
weeeen
There's nobody around...
We are Frierds!!
What a sad welcome.

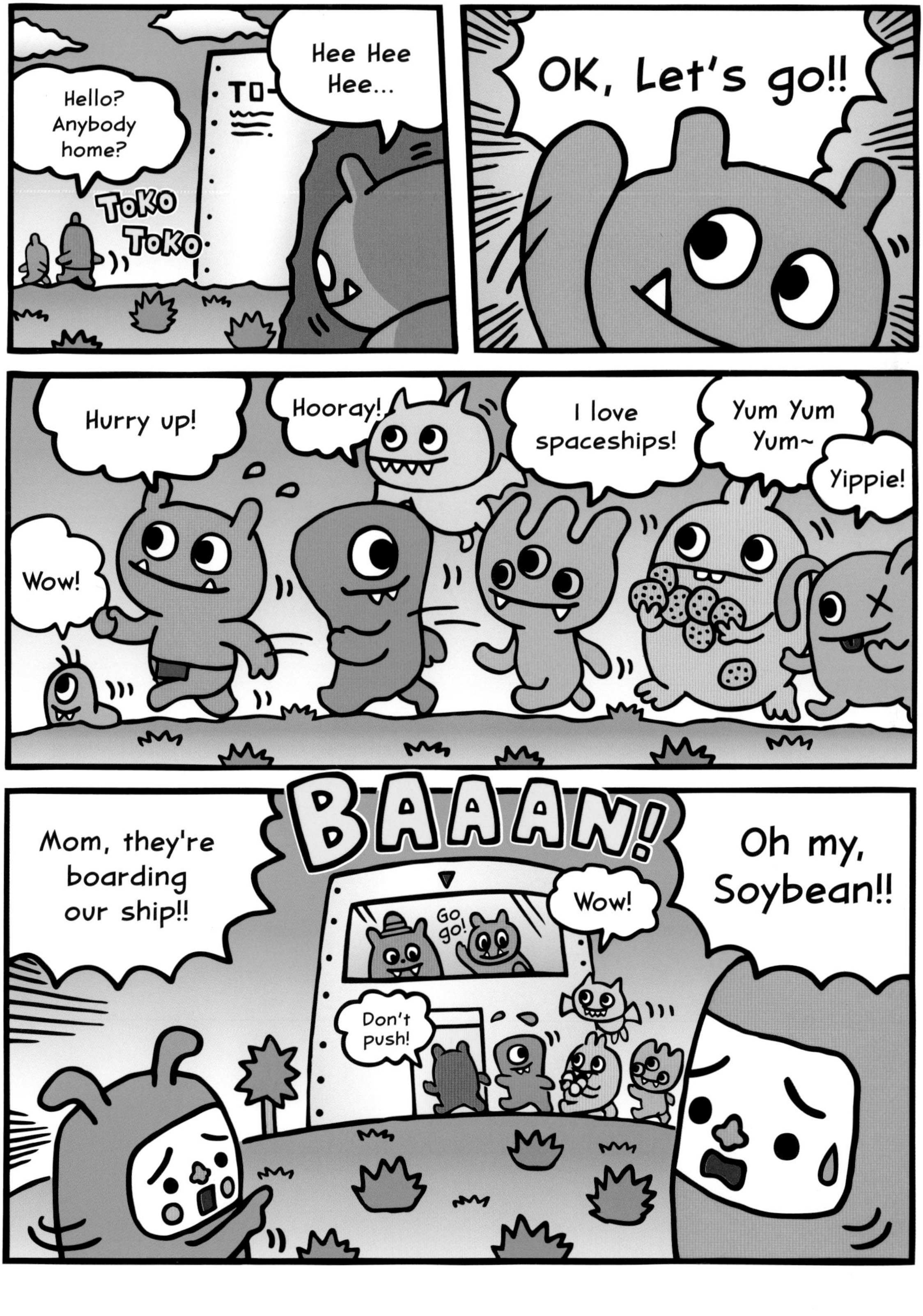
Hee Hee
Hee...
Hello?
Anybody
home?
TO-
TOKO
TOKO
OK, Let's go!!
Hurry up!
Hooray!
I love
spaceships!
Yum Yum
Yum~
Yippie!
Wow!
BAAAN!
Mom, they're
boarding
our ship!!
Oh my,
Soybean!!
Wow!
Go
go!
Don't
push!

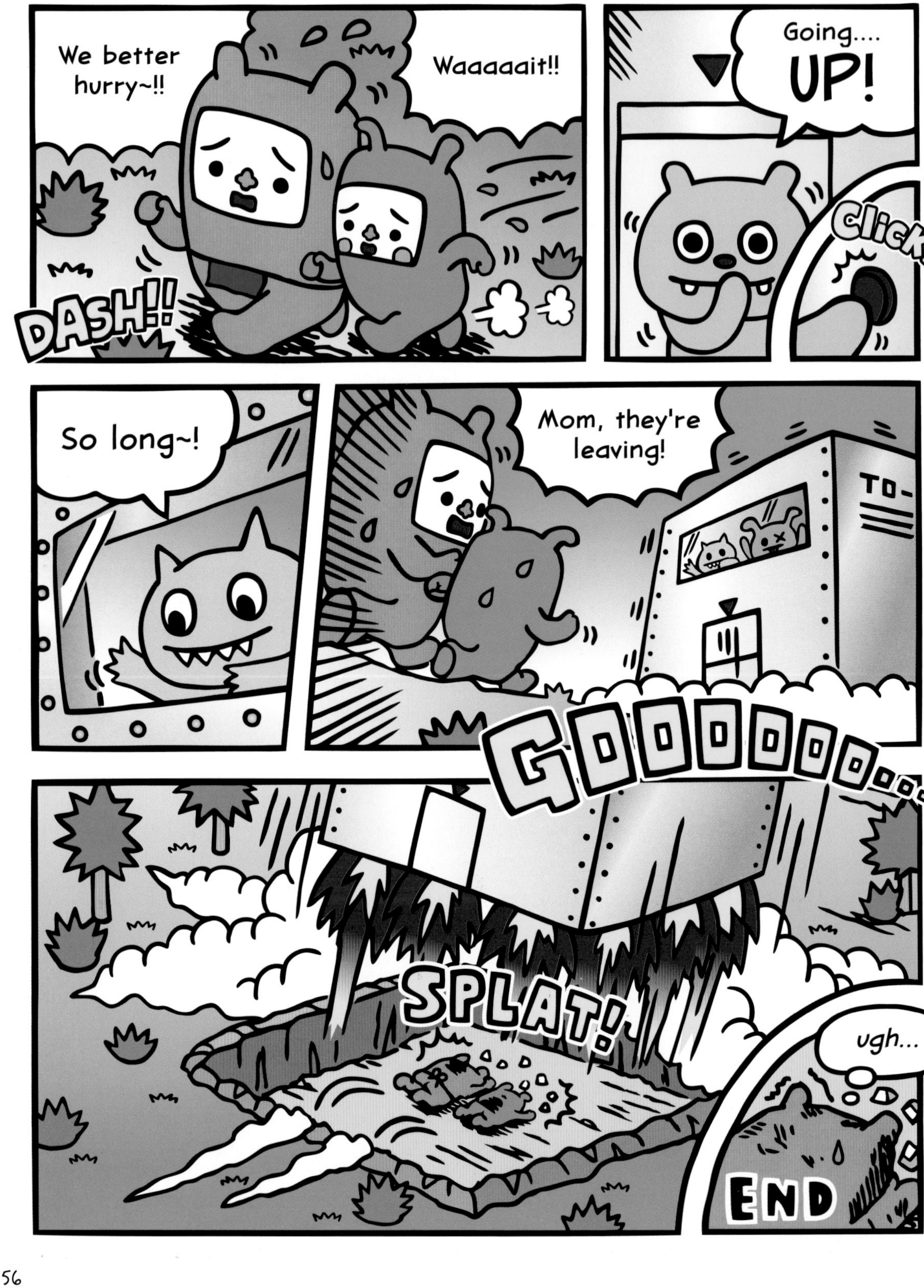

We better hurry~!!
Waaaaait!!
DASH!!
Going.... UP!
Click!
So long~!
Mom, they're leaving!
TO-
GOOOOOO...
SPLAT!
ugh...
END

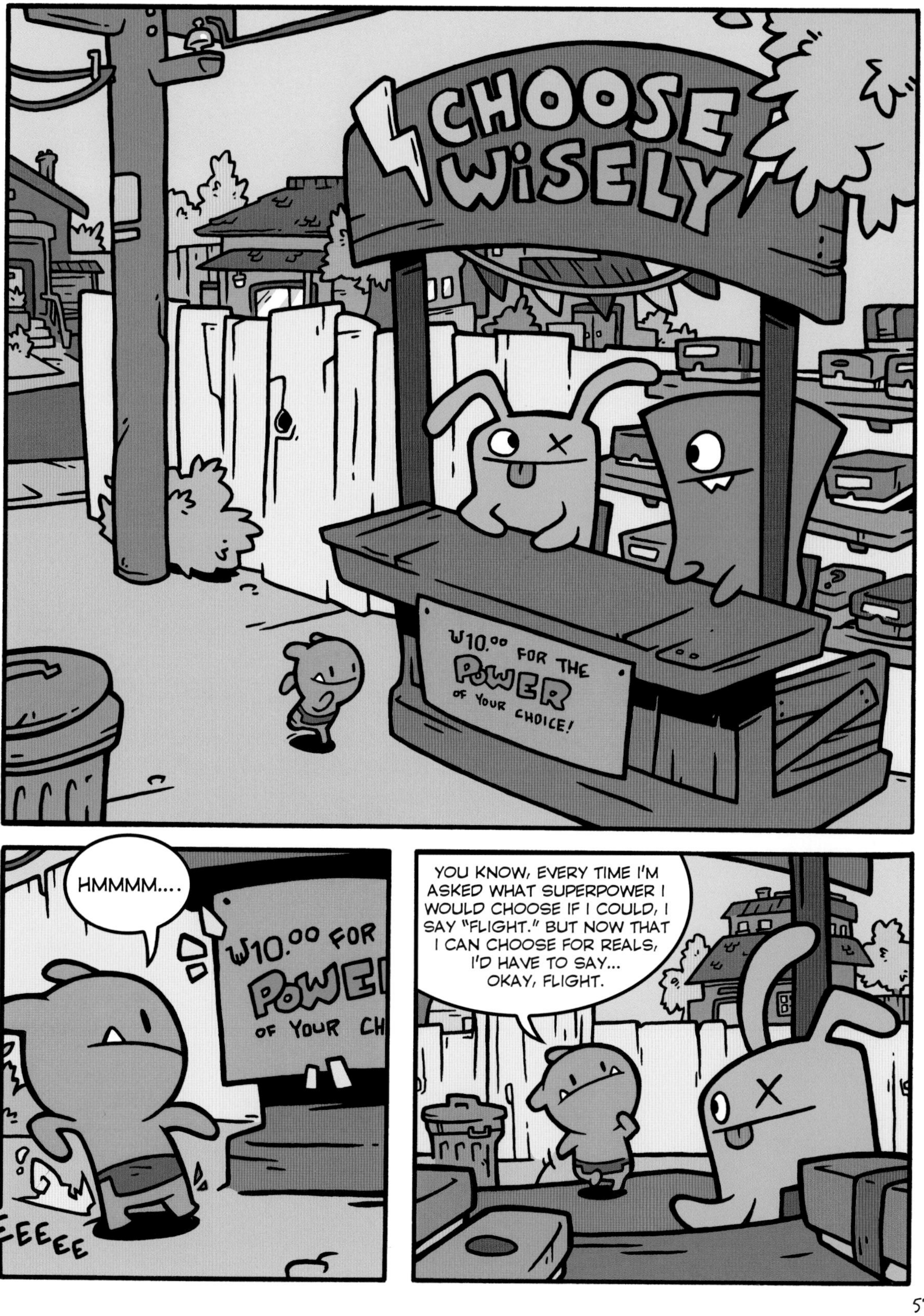
CHOOSE WISELY
₩10.00 FOR THE POWER OF YOUR CHOICE!
HMMMM....
₩10.00 FOR
OF YOUR
EEEEE
YOU KNOW, EVERY TIME I'M ASKED WHAT SUPERPOWER I WOULD CHOOSE IF I COULD, I SAY "FLIGHT." BUT NOW THAT I CAN CHOOSE FOR REALS, I'D HAVE TO SAY... OKAY, FLIGHT.

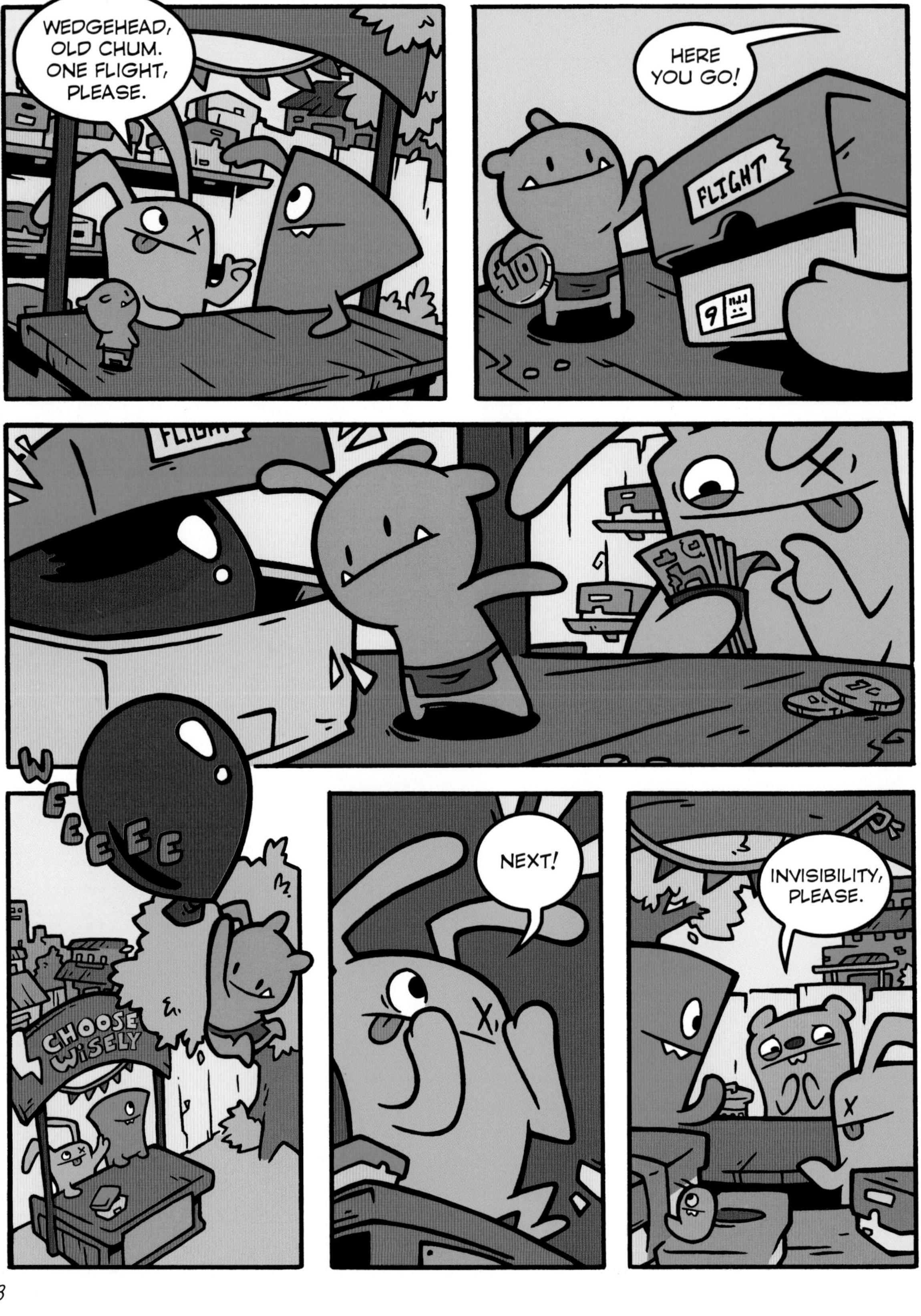
WEDGEHEAD, OLD CHUM. ONE FLIGHT, PLEASE.
HERE YOU GO!
FLIGHT
10
FLIGHT
WEEEEE
CHOOSE WISELY
NEXT!
INVISIBILITY, PLEASE.

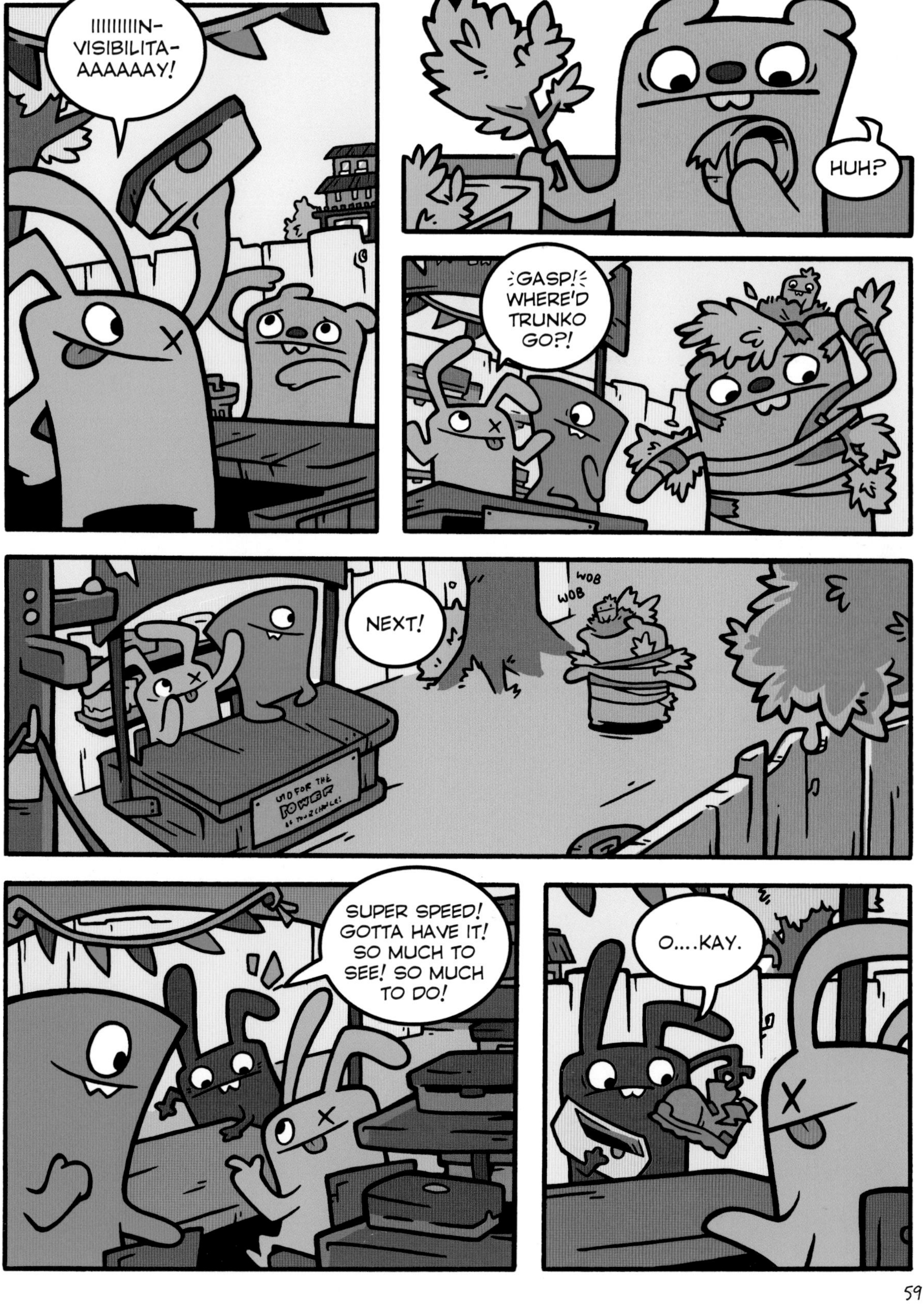

IIIIIIIIN-VISIBILITA-AAAAAAY!
HUH?
GASP! WHERE'D TRUNKO GO?!
NEXT!
WOB WOB
SUPER SPEED! GOTTA HAVE IT! SO MUCH TO SEE! SO MUCH TO DO!
O....KAY.

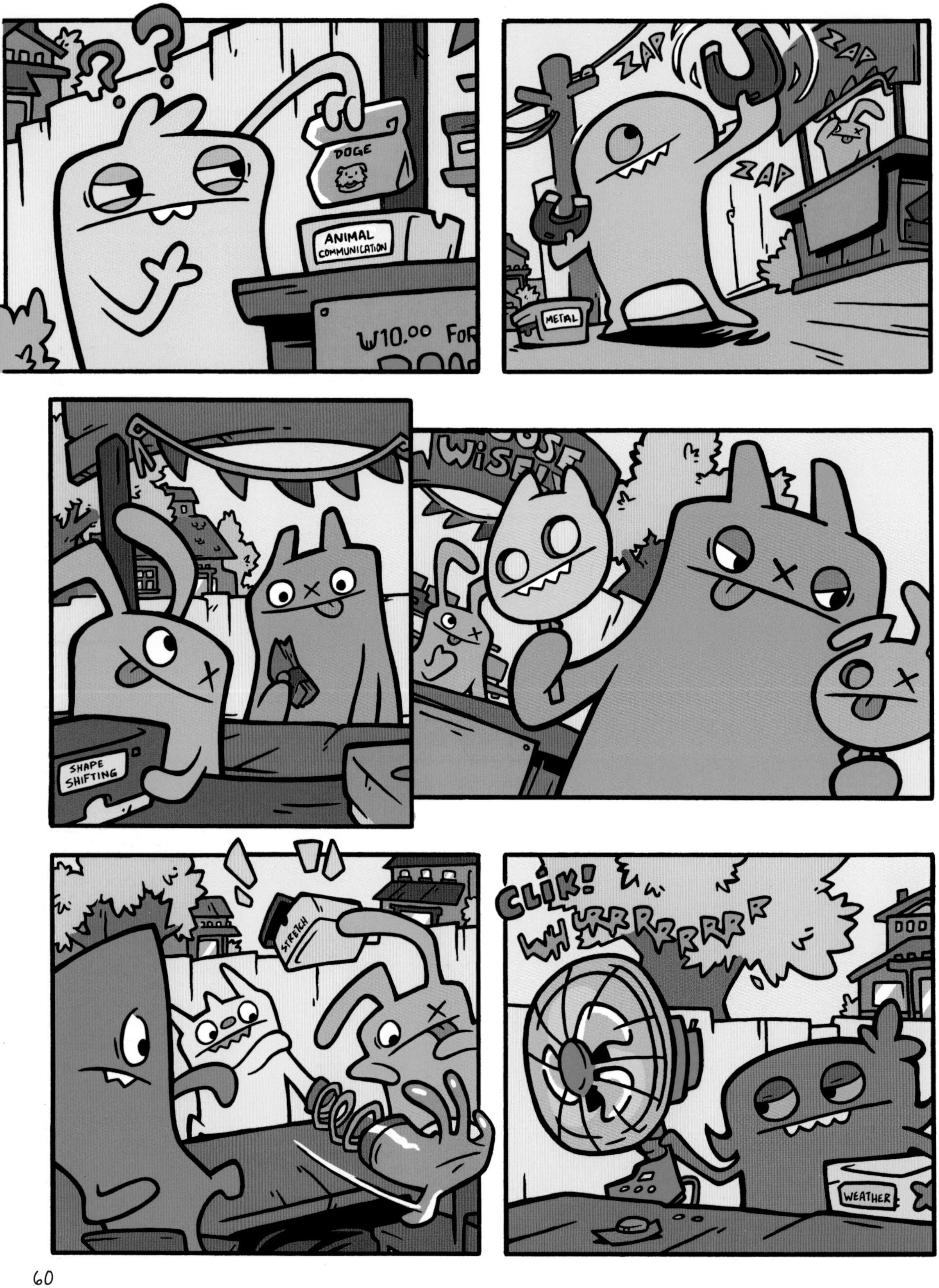
DOGE
ANIMAL COMMUNICATION
₩10.00 FOR
ZAP
ZAP
ZAP
METAL
SHAPE SHIFTING
STRETCH
CLIK!
WHURRRRRRRR
WEATHER

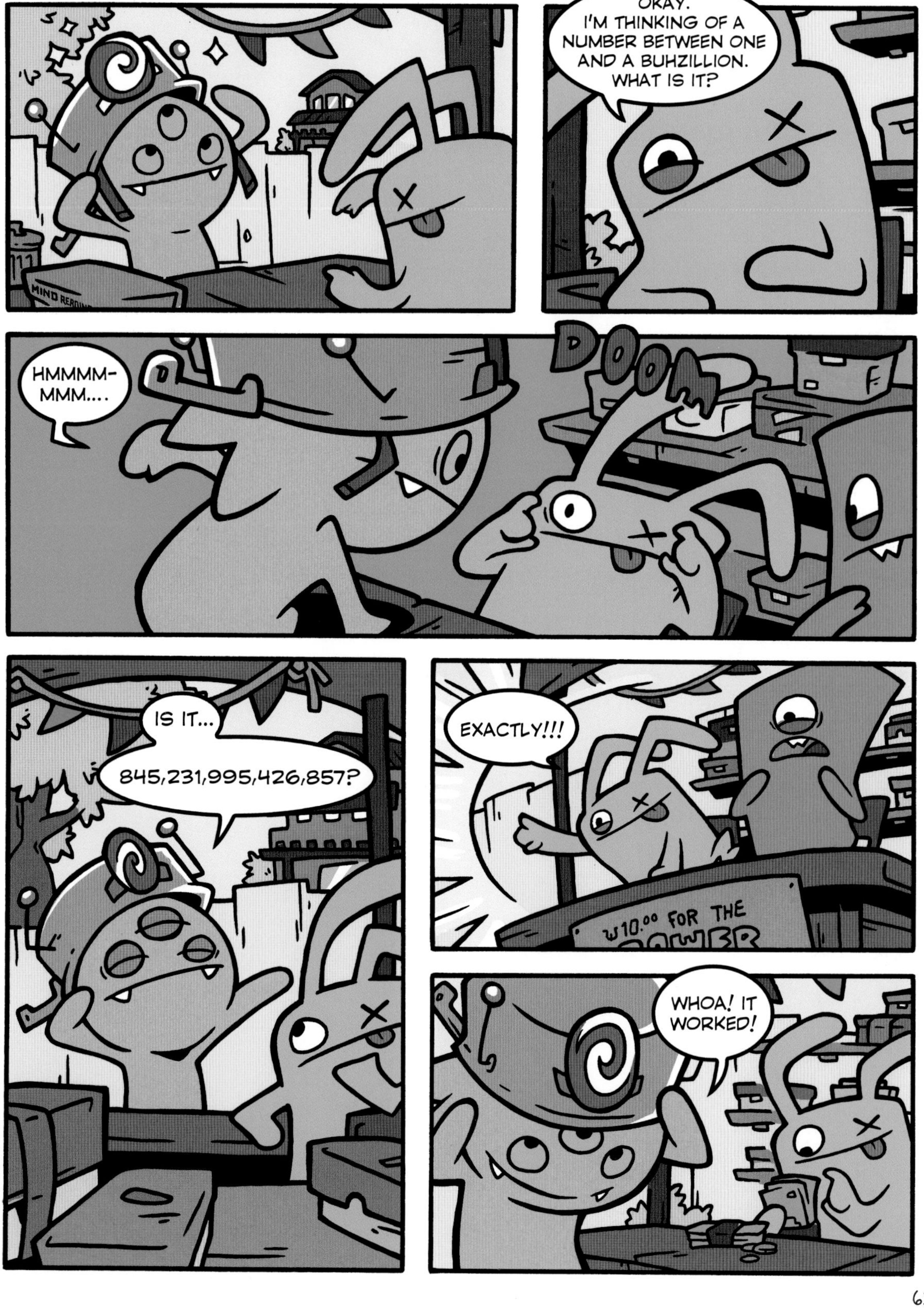
MIND READING
OKAY. I'M THINKING OF A NUMBER BETWEEN ONE AND A BUHZILLION. WHAT IS IT?
HMMMM-MMM....
DOOM
IS IT...
845,231,995,426,857?
EXACTLY!!!
W10.00 FOR THE
WHOA! IT WORKED!

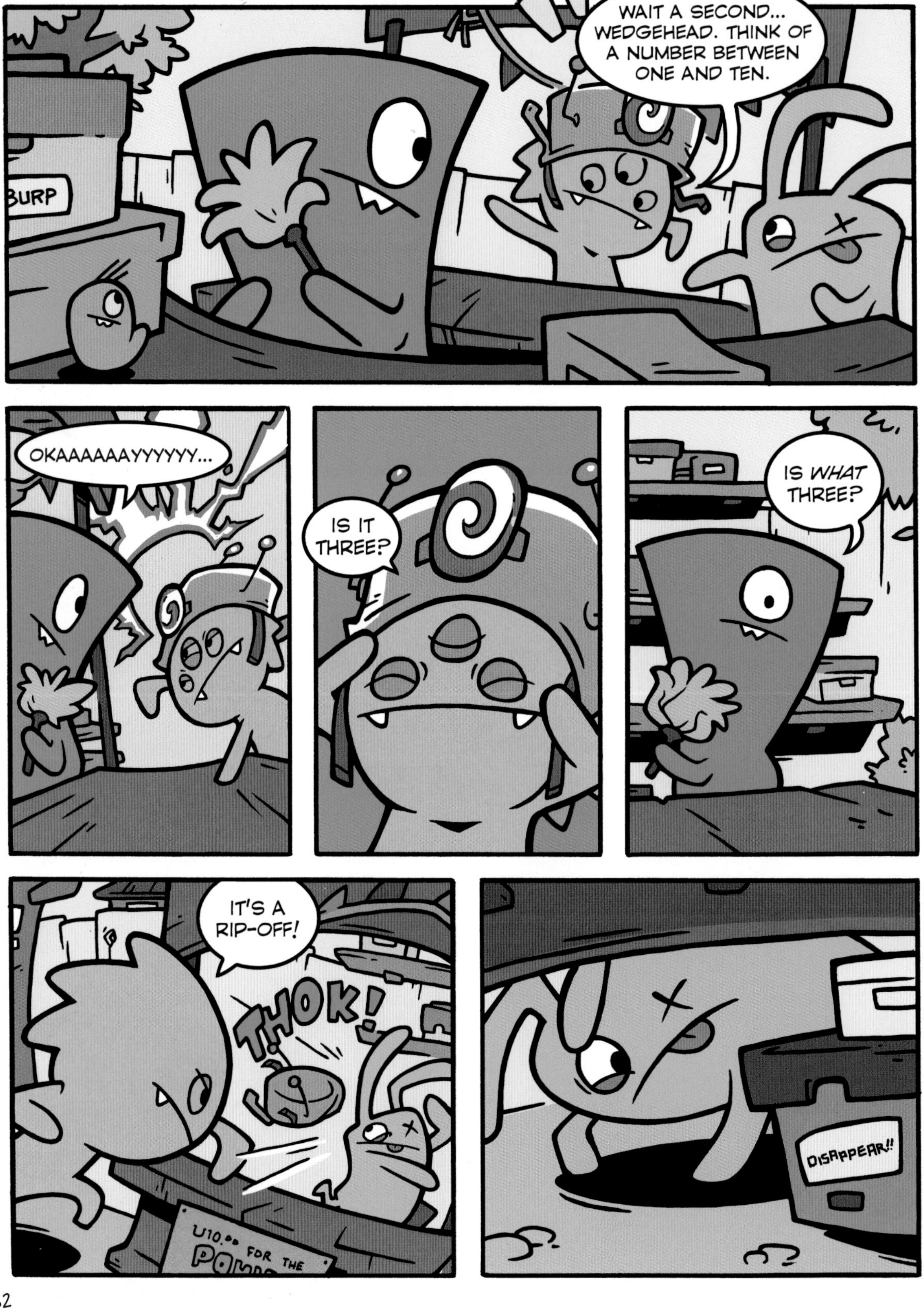
BURP
WAIT A SECOND... WEDGEHEAD. THINK OF A NUMBER BETWEEN ONE AND TEN.
OKAAAAAAYYYYYY...
IS IT THREE?
IS *WHAT* THREE?
IT'S A RIP-OFF!
THOK!
U10.00 FOR THE
DISAPPEAR!!

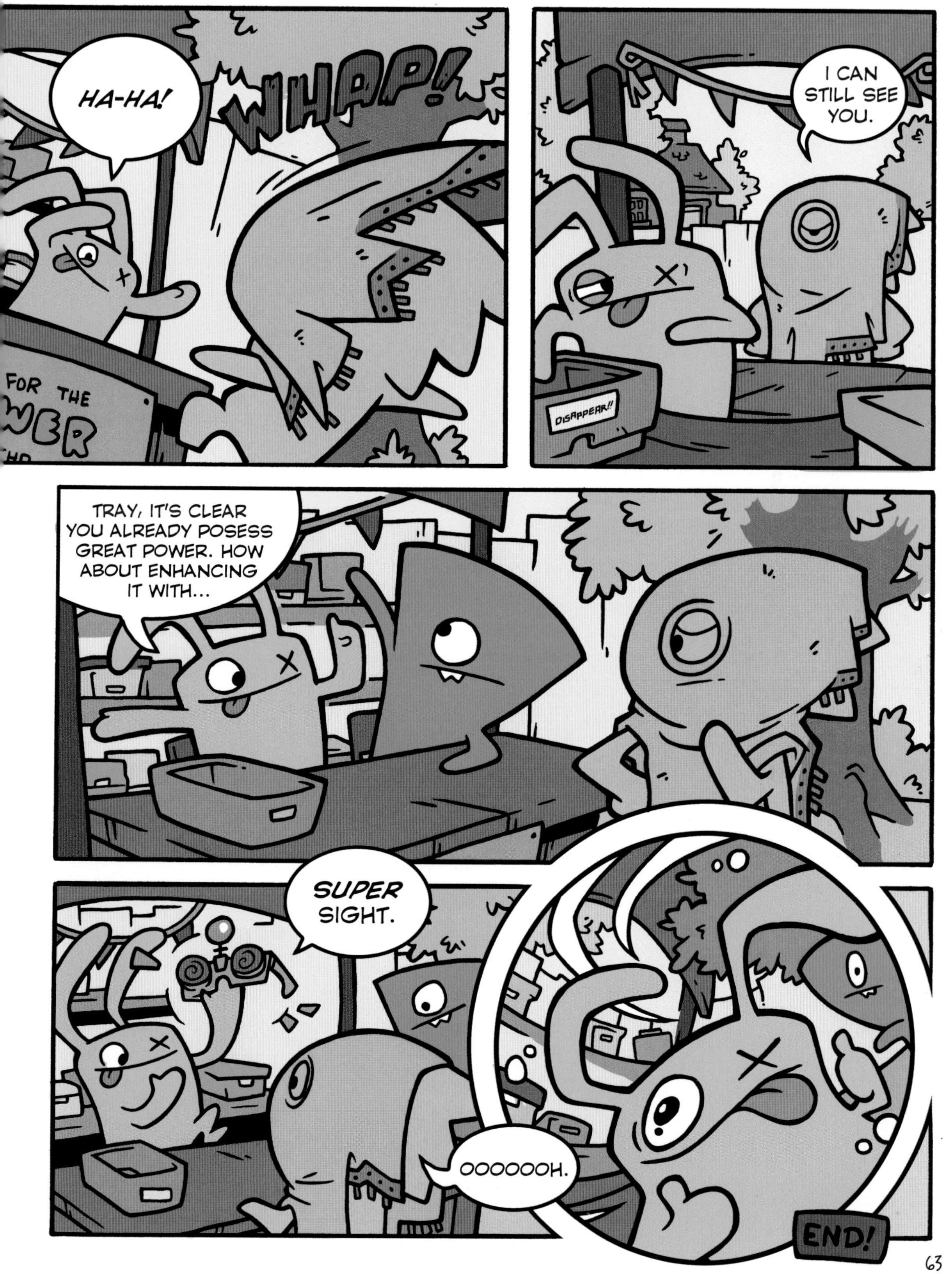
HA-HA!
WHAP!
FOR THE
WER
I CAN STILL SEE YOU.
DISAPPEAR!!
TRAY, IT'S CLEAR YOU ALREADY POSESS GREAT POWER. HOW ABOUT ENHANCING IT WITH...
SUPER SIGHT.
OOOOOOH.
END!

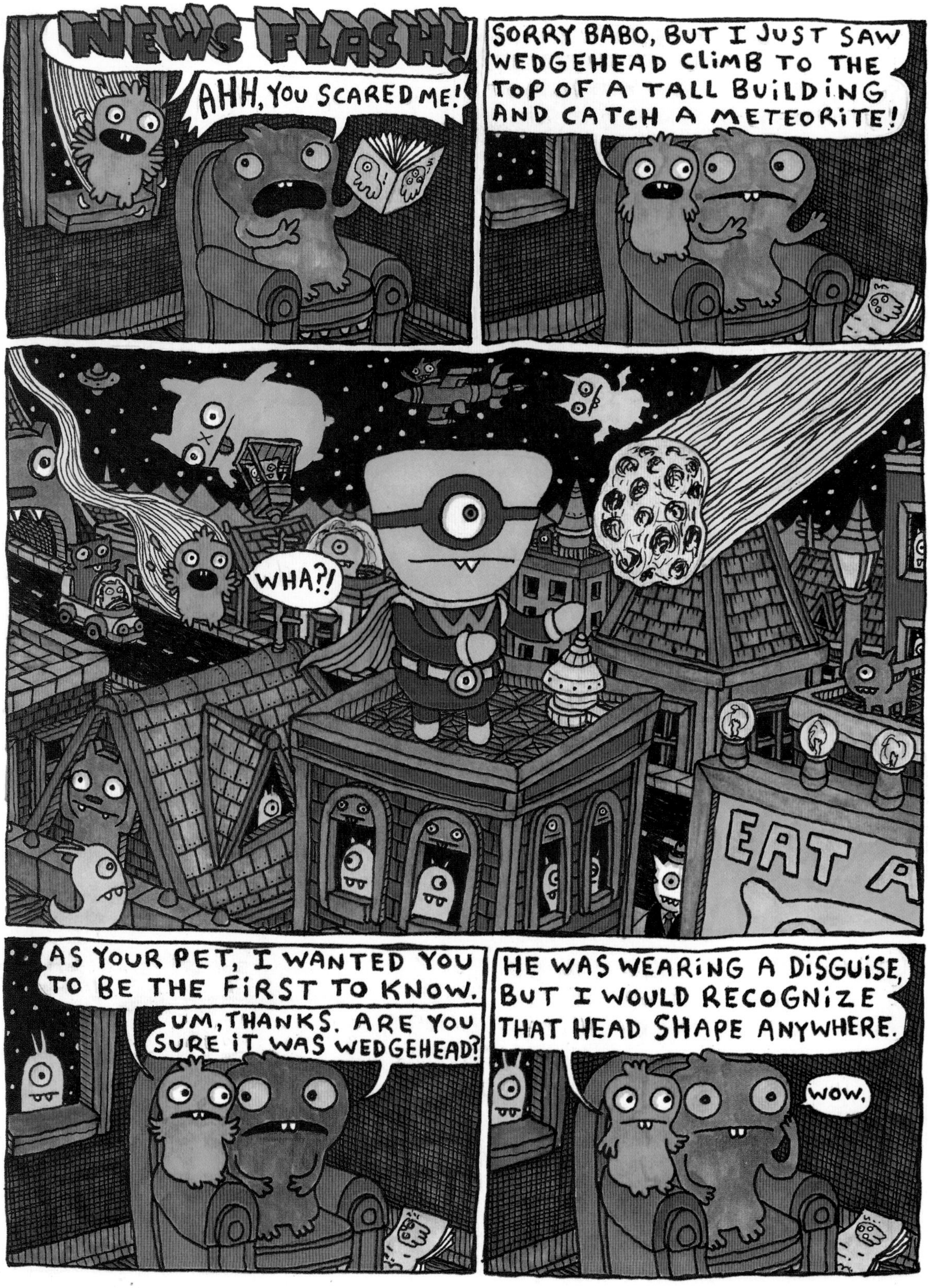
NEWS FLASH!
AHH, YOU SCARED ME!
SORRY BABO, BUT I JUST SAW WEDGEHEAD CLIMB TO THE TOP OF A TALL BUILDING AND CATCH A METEORITE!
WHA?!
EAT A
AS YOUR PET, I WANTED YOU TO BE THE FIRST TO KNOW.
UM, THANKS. ARE YOU SURE IT WAS WEDGEHEAD?
HE WAS WEARING A DISGUISE, BUT I WOULD RECOGNIZE THAT HEAD SHAPE ANYWHERE.
WOW.

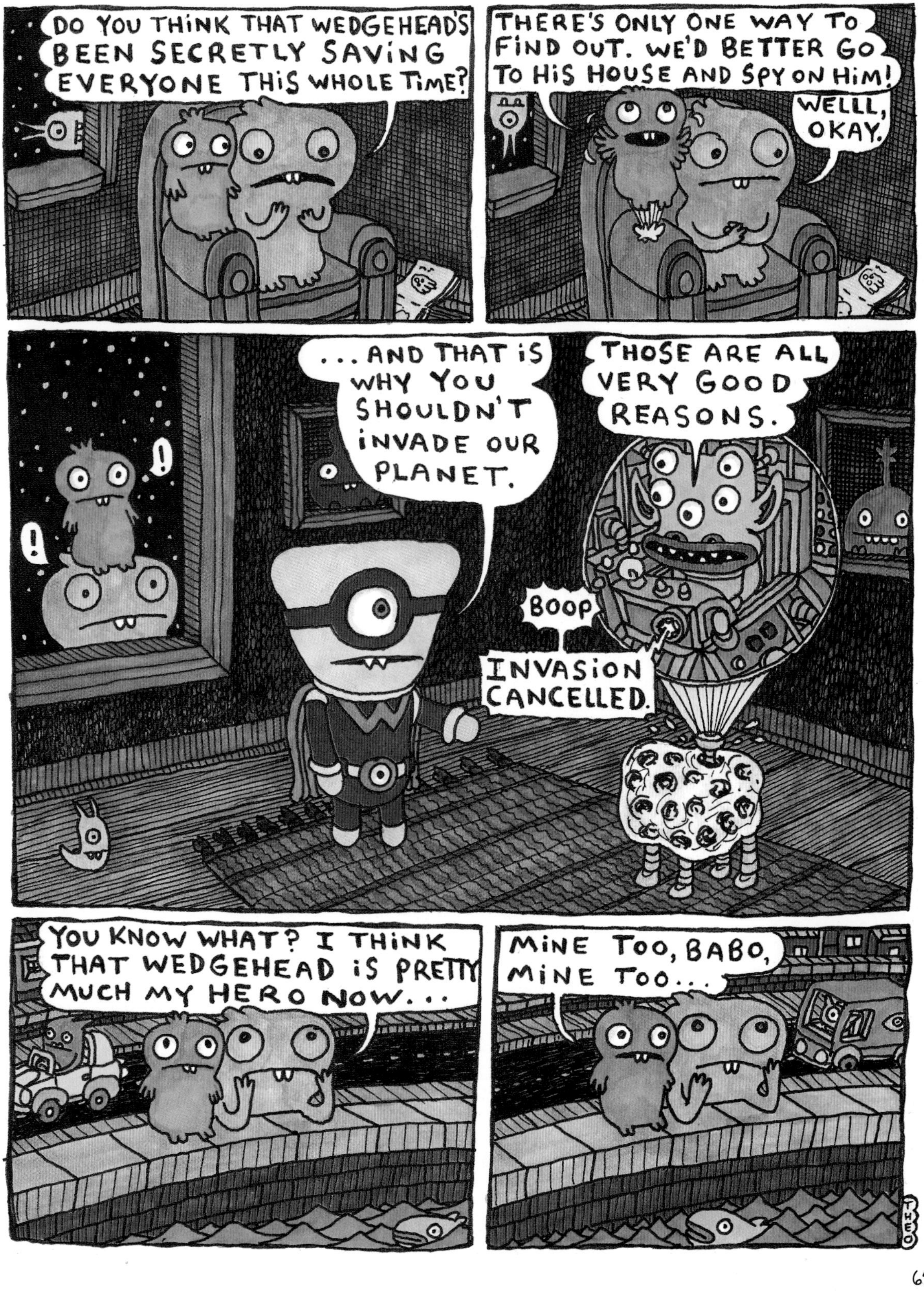
DO YOU THINK THAT WEDGEHEAD'S BEEN SECRETLY SAVING EVERYONE THIS WHOLE TIME?
THERE'S ONLY ONE WAY TO FIND OUT. WE'D BETTER GO TO HIS HOUSE AND SPY ON HIM!
WELLL, OKAY.
!
!
...AND THAT IS WHY YOU SHOULDN'T INVADE OUR PLANET.
THOSE ARE ALL VERY GOOD REASONS.
BOOP
INVASION CANCELLED.
YOU KNOW WHAT? I THINK THAT WEDGEHEAD IS PRETTY MUCH MY HERO NOW...
MINE TOO, BABO, MINE TOO...
THEO

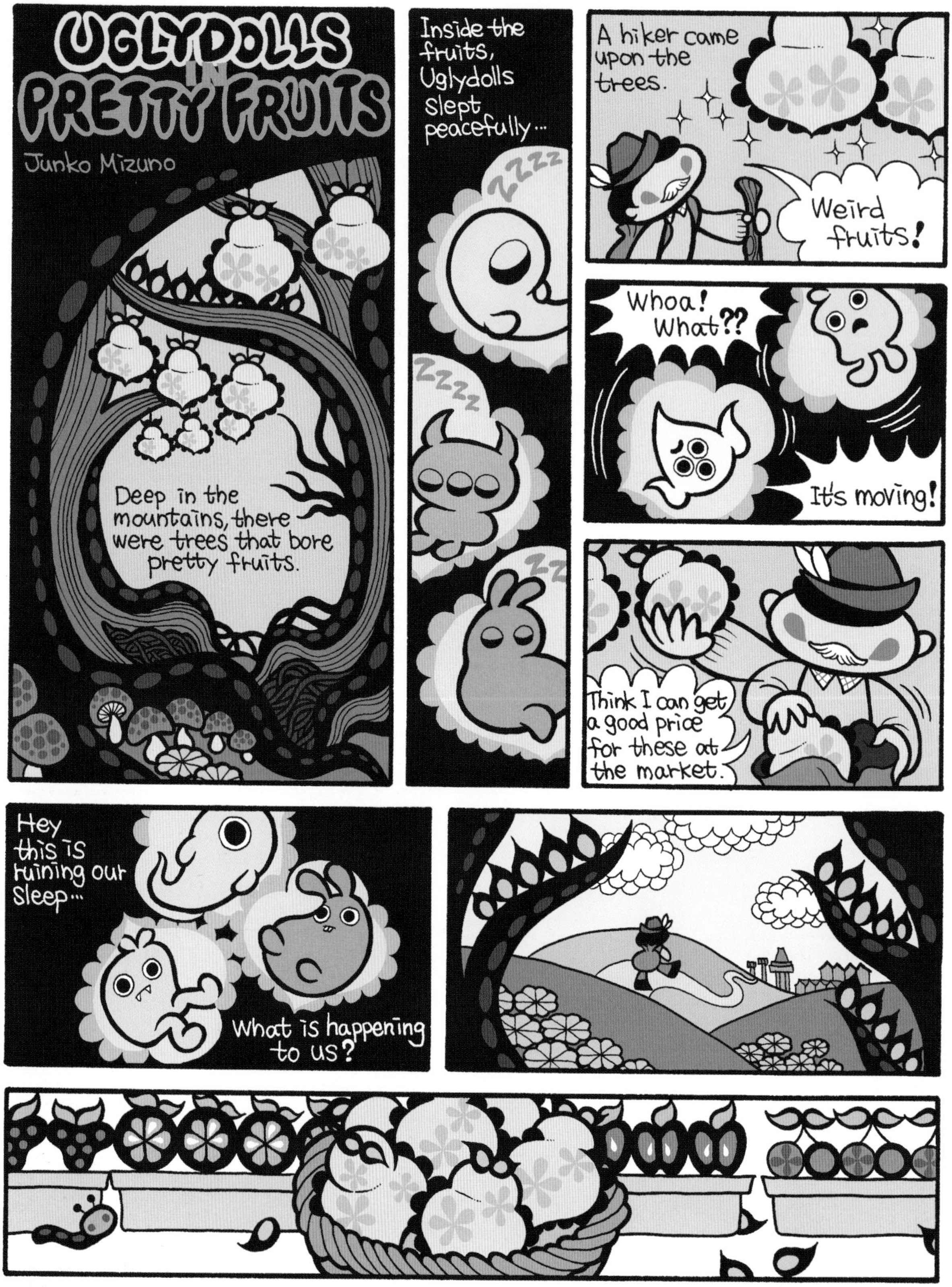
UGLYDOLLS IN PRETTY FRUITS
Junko Mizuno
Deep in the mountains, there were trees that bore pretty fruits.
Inside the fruits, Uglydolls slept peacefully...
ZZZZ
ZZZZ
ZZ
A hiker came upon the trees.
Weird fruits!
Whoa! What??
It's moving!
Think I can get a good price for these at the market.
Hey this is ruining our sleep...
What is happening to us?

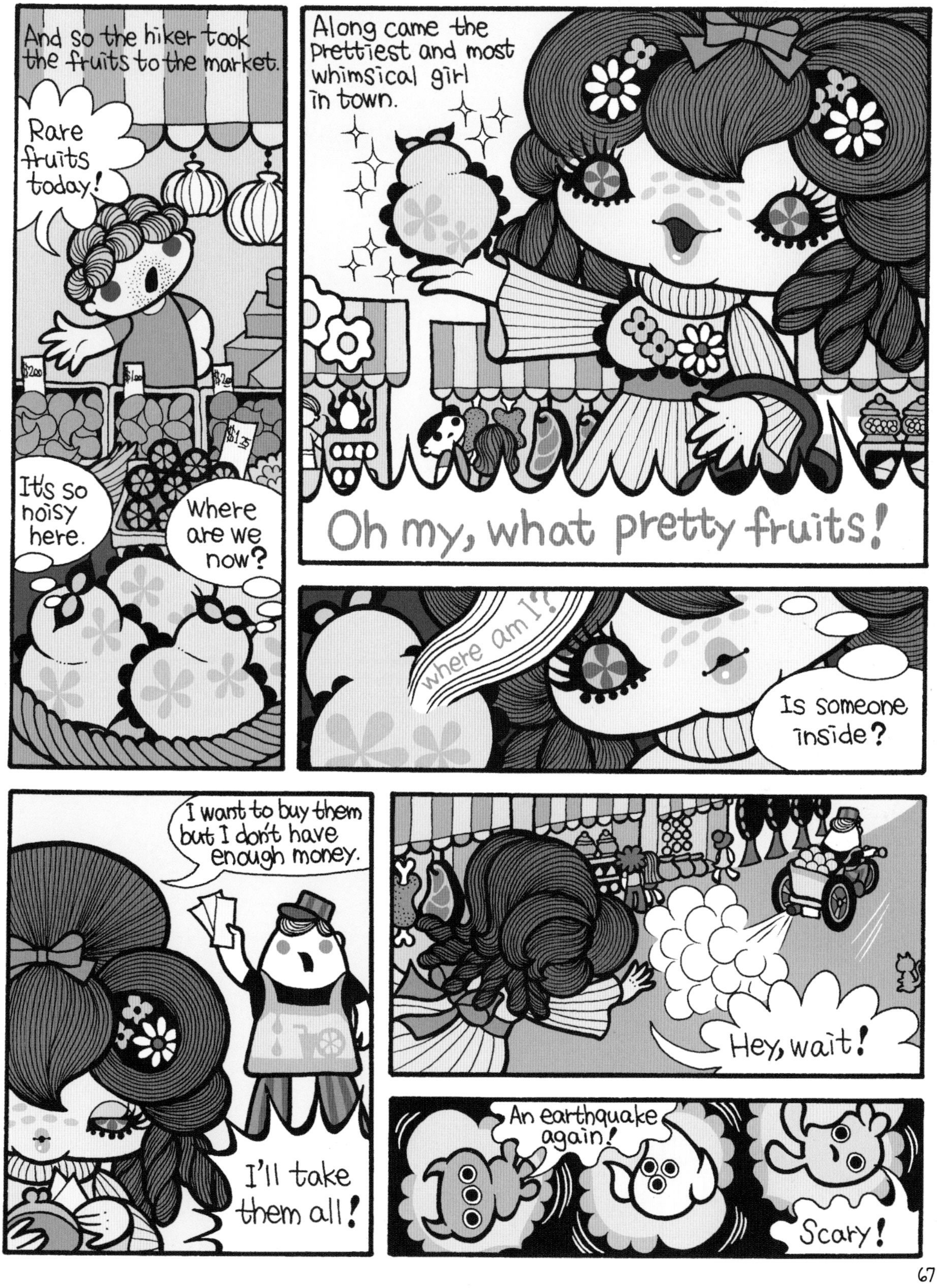
And so the hiker took the fruits to the market.
Rare fruits today!
$2.00
$1.00
$2.00
$1.25
It's so noisy here.
Where are we now?
Along came the prettiest and most whimsical girl in town.
Oh my, what pretty fruits!
Where am I?
Is someone inside?
I want to buy them but I don't have enough money.
I'll take them all!
Hey, wait!
An earthquake again!
Scary!

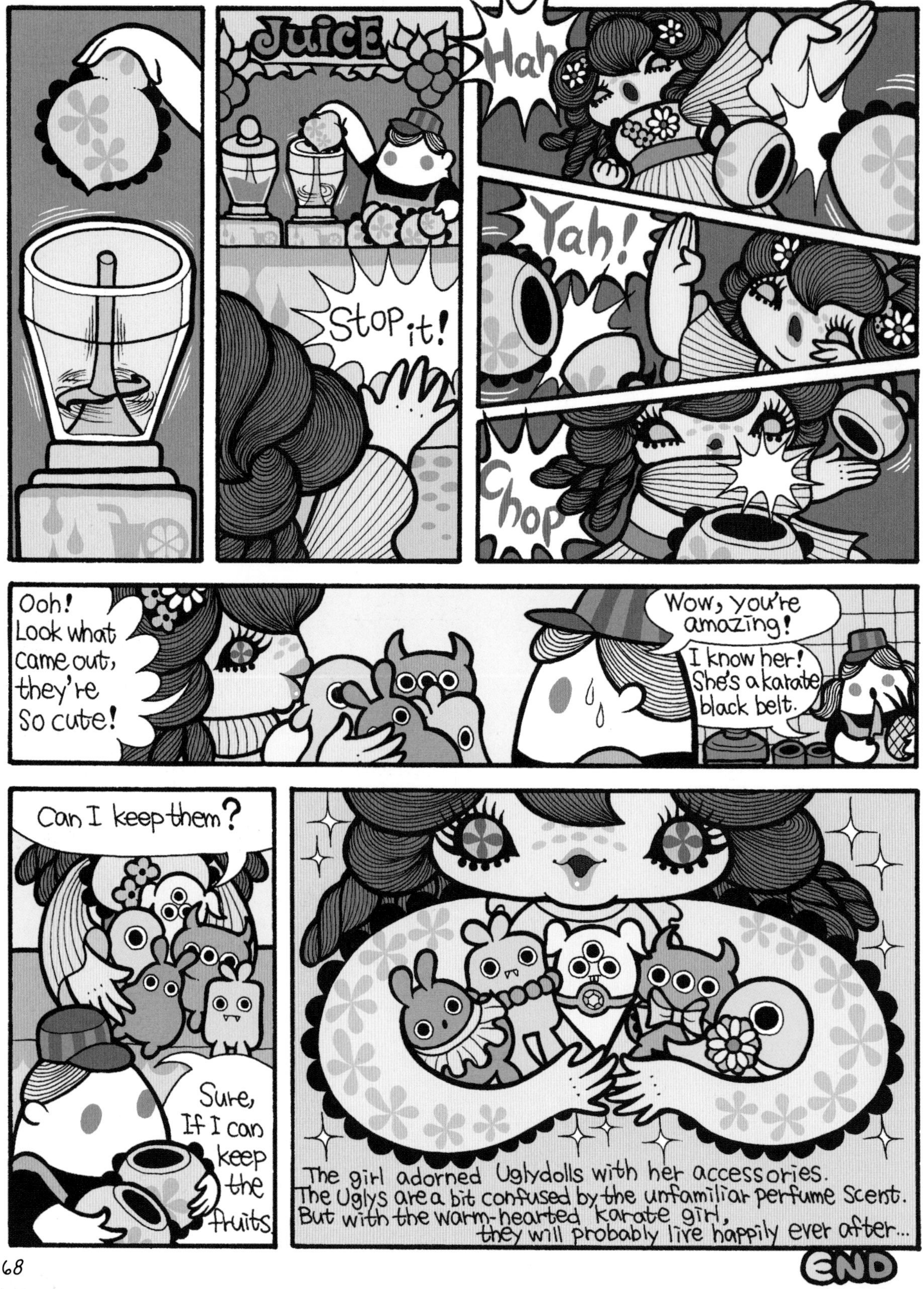

JUICE
Stop it!
Hah
Yah!
Chop
Ooh! Look what came out, they're so cute!
Wow, you're amazing!
I know her! She's a karate black belt.
Can I keep them?
Sure, If I can keep the fruits.
The girl adorned Uglydolls with her accessories.
The Uglys are a bit confused by the unfamiliar perfume scent.
But with the warm-hearted karate girl,
they will probably live happily ever after...
END

BE a HERO

Create your own Heroic Uglyverse story with help from this chance-a-rific chart! All you need is a six-sided die from a board game, some paper, and something to write with. Roll the die for each step and write down the results. Then create your story!

THE HEROIC:

1. Babo
2. Ox
3 Ice-Bat
4. Tray
5. Wage
6. Wedgehead

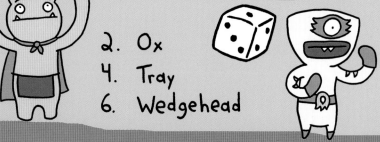

WITH THEIR POWER OF:

1. Super whistle
2. Realization they're in a story
3. Talking to dirt
4. Atomic guitar solos
5. Unlimited chocolate chips
6. Super stretchy tongue

AND HELP FROM THEIR SIDEKICK:

1. A potted plant
2. Babo's Bird
3. A swarm of tiny Jeeros
4. A version of himself/herself from the future
5. Cinko, who refuses to leave the hideout
6. A talking ball of cookie dough

BATTLE THE EVIL:

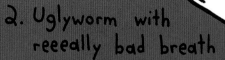

1. Team of noodle-wielding ninjas
2. Uglyworm with reeeally bad breath
3. Opposite-universe Wage
4. Sock puppet with a bad attitude
5. Robo-Tacos
6. Overdue library book

AT/ON/IN:

1. The Age of Futuristic Dinosaurs!
2. An arena on Planet Q!
3. An abandoned amusement park!
4. A really long movie line.
5. A really boring island.
6. The whole stinking 'verse!

Now that you've got your story elements, write/draw your story! And don't feel limited to these choices. You have the power of
SUPER IMAGINATION!

TRACY NICHOLS

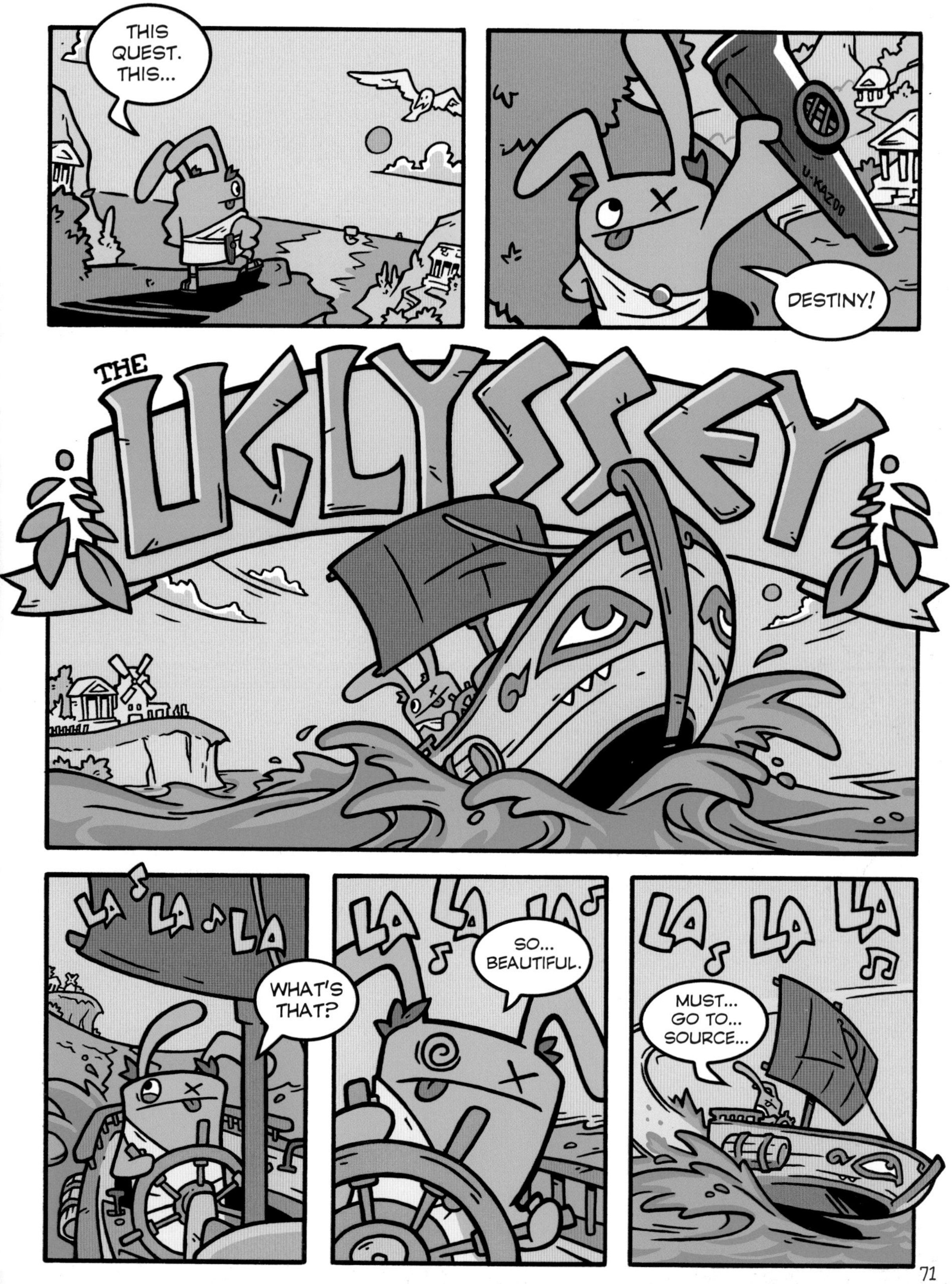

THIS QUEST. THIS...
U-KAZOO
DESTINY!
THE UGLYSSEY
LA LA LA
WHAT'S THAT?
LA LA LA
SO... BEAUTIFUL.
LA LA LA
MUST... GO TO... SOURCE...

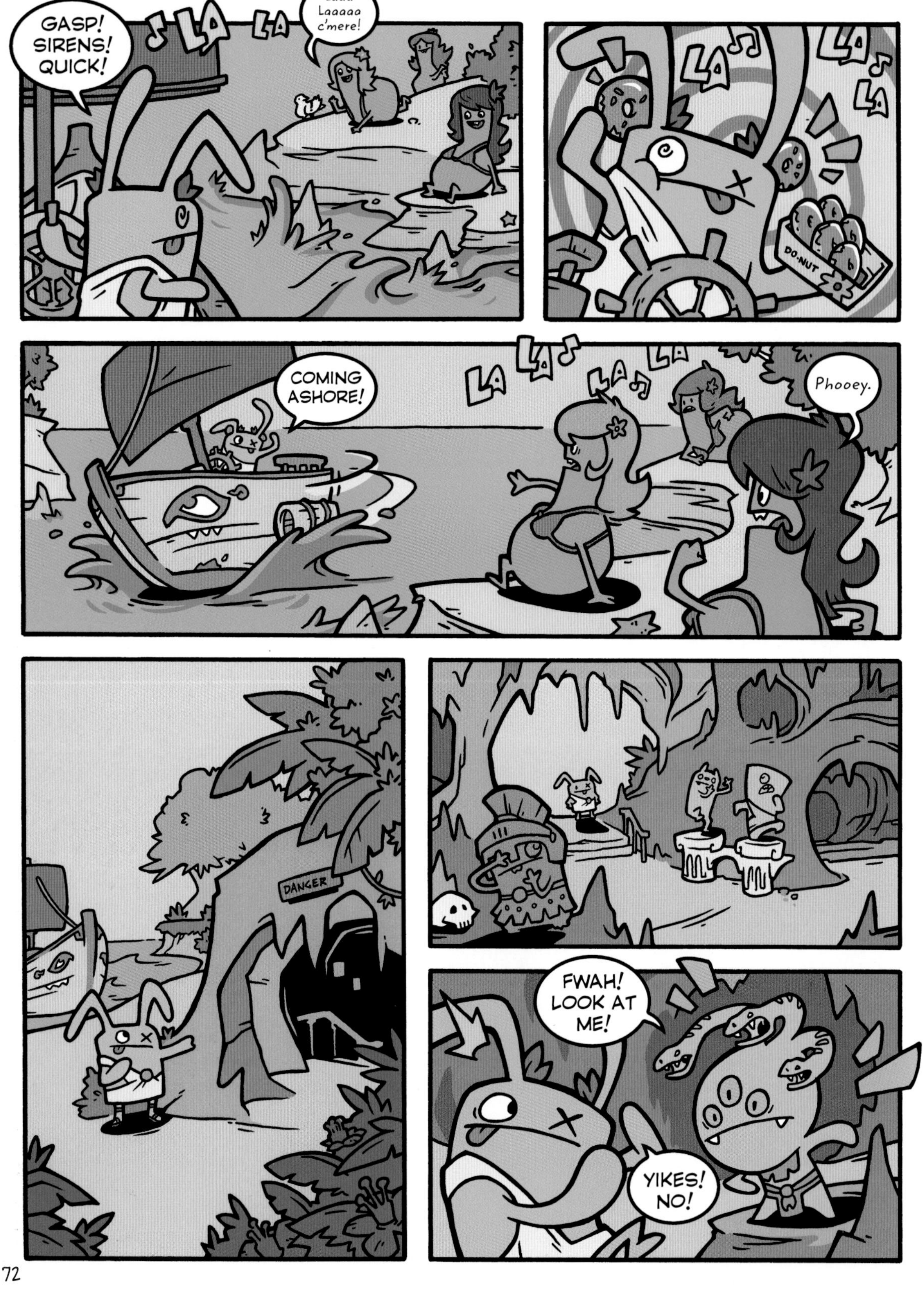
GASP! SIRENS! QUICK!
LA LA
Laaa Laaaaa c'mere!
LA LA LA
COMING ASHORE!
LA LA LA LA
Phooey.
DO-NUT
DANGER
FWAH! LOOK AT ME!
YIKES! NO!

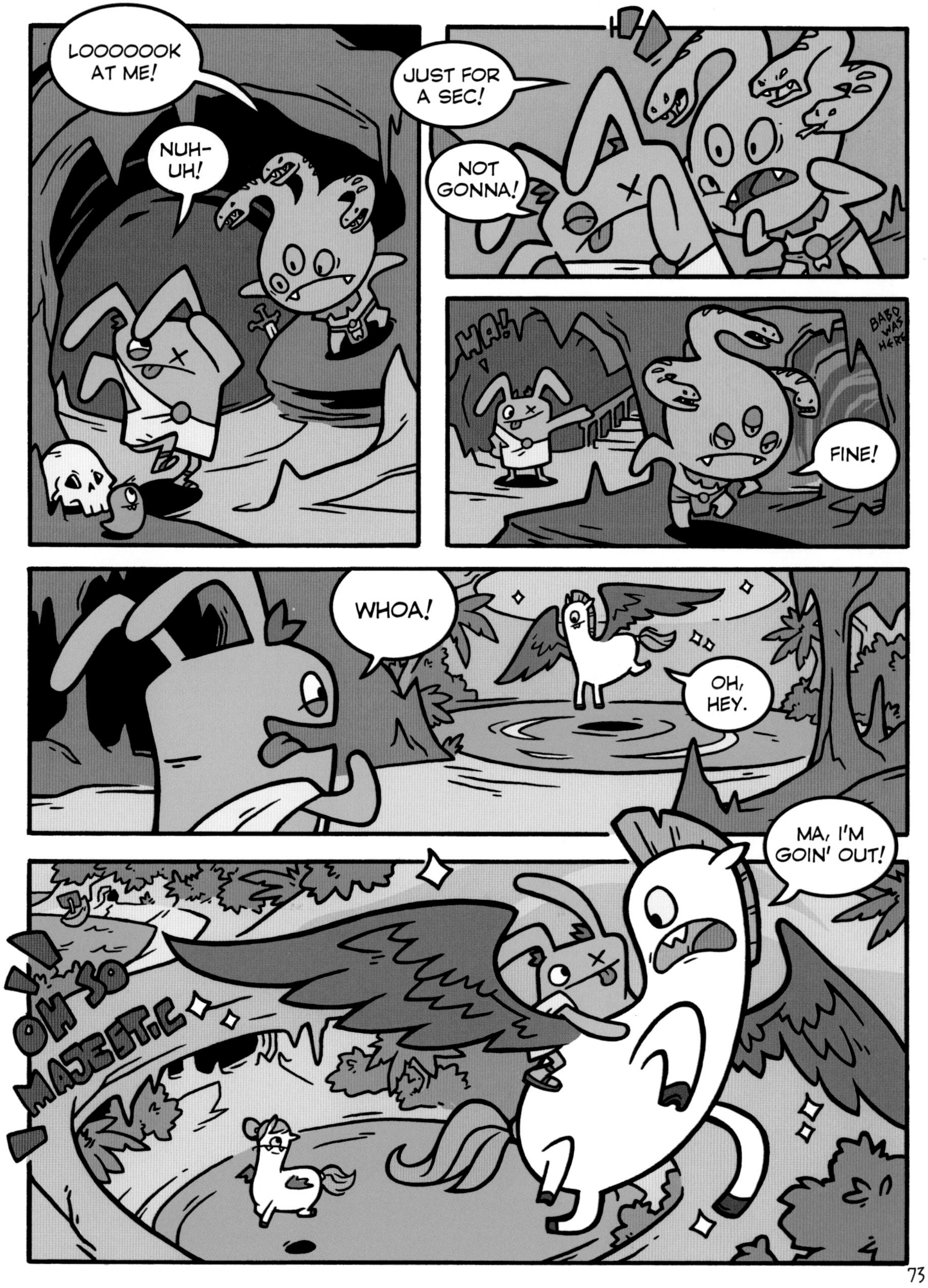
LOOOOOOK AT ME!
NUH-UH!
JUST FOR A SEC!
NOT GONNA!
HA!
BABO WAS HERE
FINE!
WHOA!
OH, HEY.
MA, I'M GOIN' OUT!
OH SO MAJESTIC

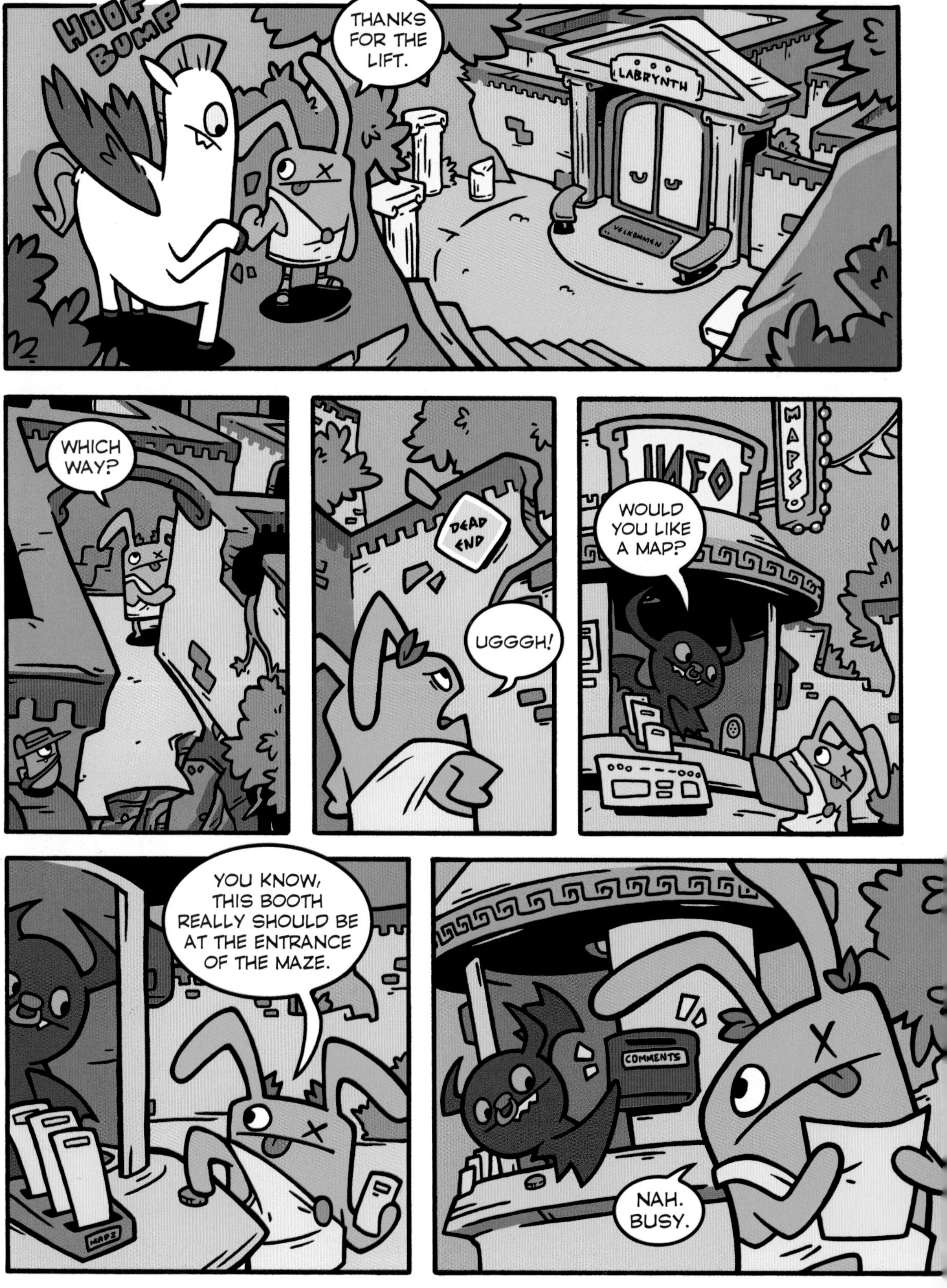
HOOF BUMP
THANKS FOR THE LIFT.
LABRYNTH
VELKOMMEN
WHICH WAY?
DEAD END
UGGGH!
INFO
MAPS
WOULD YOU LIKE A MAP?
YOU KNOW, THIS BOOTH REALLY SHOULD BE AT THE ENTRANCE OF THE MAZE.
COMMENTS
NAH. BUSY.

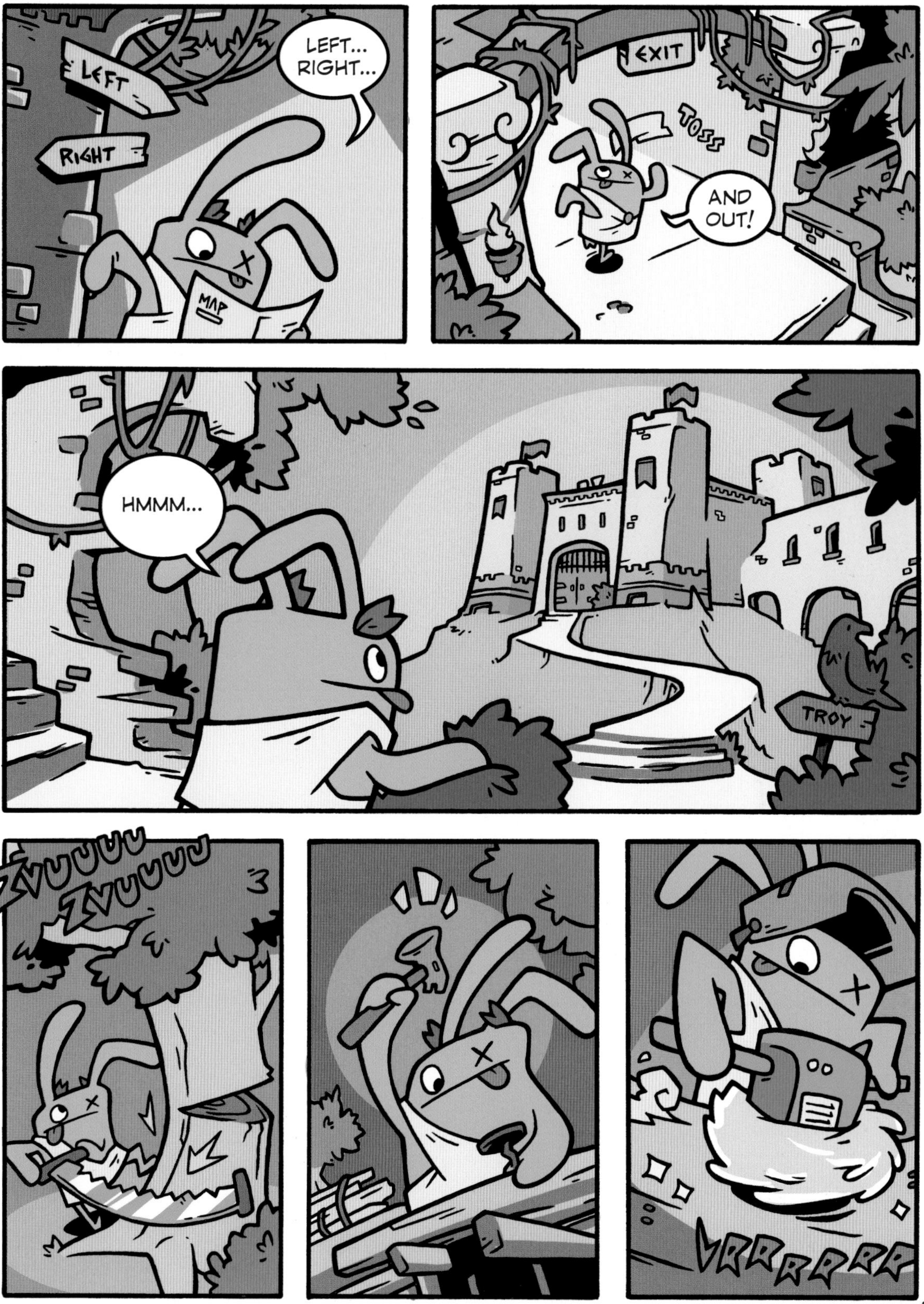
LEFT
RIGHT
LEFT... RIGHT...
MAP
EXIT
TOSS
AND OUT!
HMMM...
TROY
ZVUUUU ZVUUUU
VRRRRRR

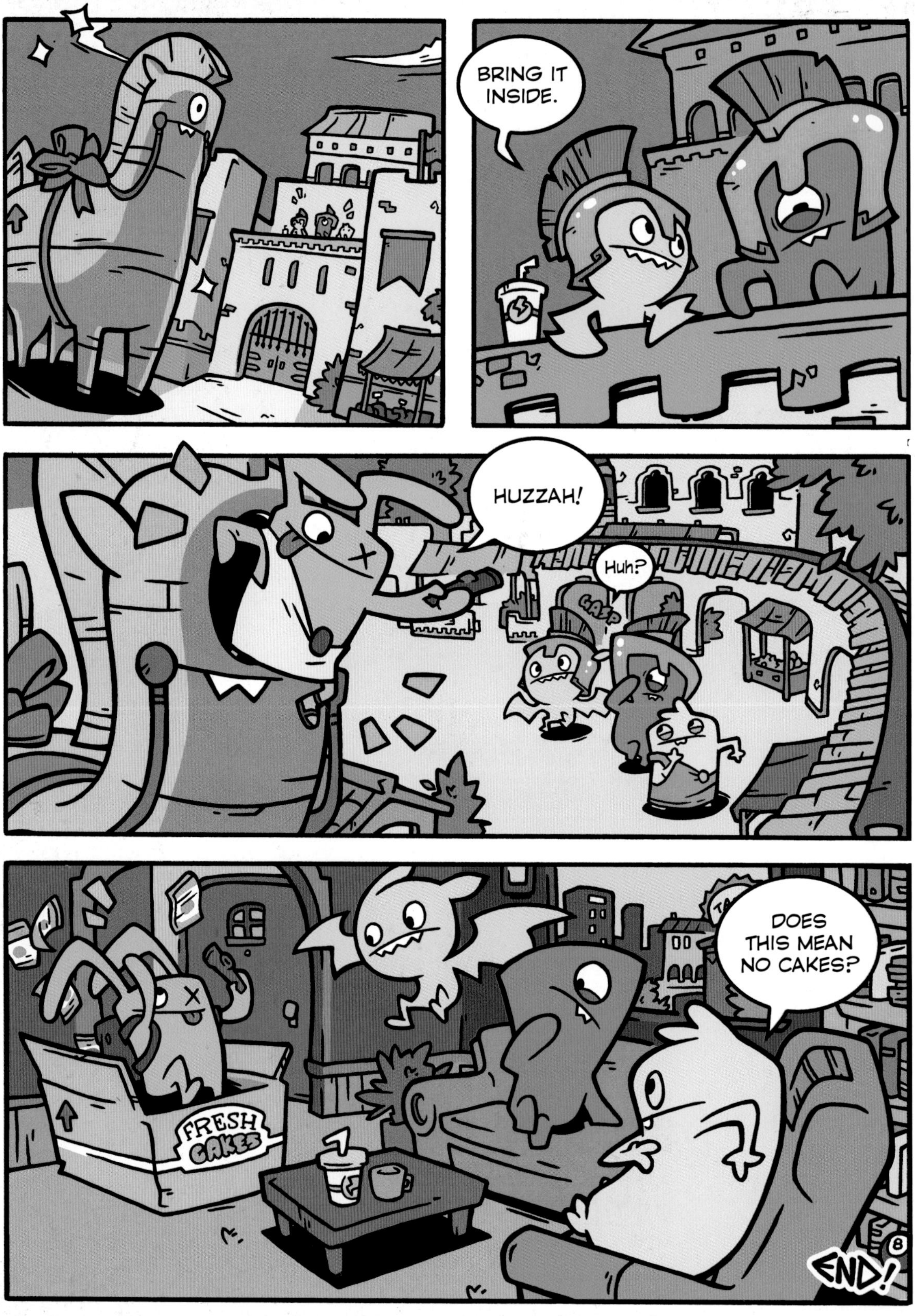
BRING IT INSIDE.
HUZZAH!
Huh?
GASP
FRESH CAKES
DOES THIS MEAN NO CAKES?
END!
8

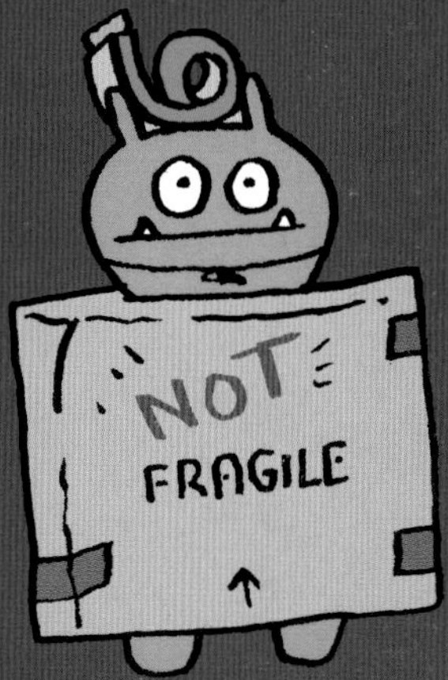
NOT
FRAGILE

BROUGHT

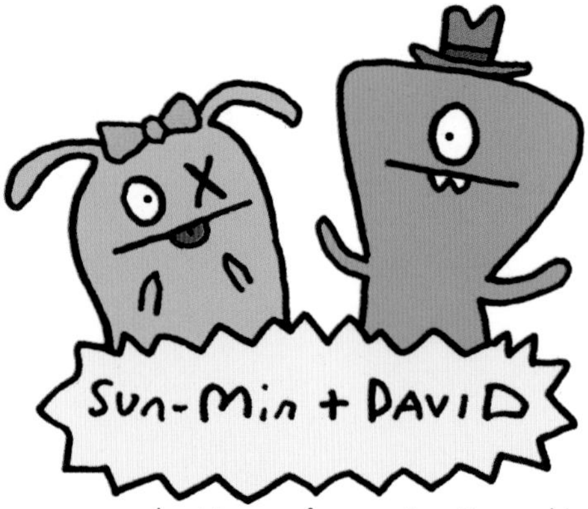
Sun-Min + DAVID

SUN-MIN KIM & DAVID HORVATH

are best known for creating the world of Uglydoll, which started as a line of handmade plush dolls and has since grown into a brand loved by all ages around the world. Their works can be found everywhere from the Moma in Tokyo and the Louvre in Paris, to the windows of their very own Uglydoll shop in Seoul. Sun-Min and David's very first conversation was about the meaning of "ugly." To them, ugly means unique and different, that which makes us who we are. It should never be hidden, but shouted from the rooftops! They wanted to build a world that showed the twists and turns that make us who we are, inside and out, because the whole world benefits when we embrace our true, twisty-turny selves. So, ugly is the new beauty. This Uglydoll comic features some of Sun-Min and David's heroes from the pop art and comic art world.

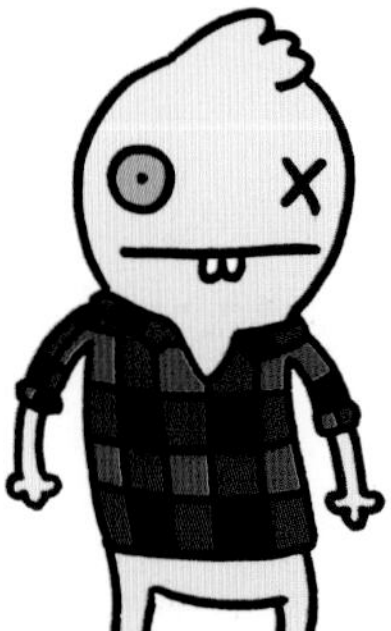

TRAVIS NICHOLS

is the author and illustrator of several books for kids and post-kids, including *The Monster Doodle Book*, *Punk Rock Etiquette* and *Matthew Meets the Man*. He previously drew comics for the late, great *Nickelodeon Magazine*. His deepest, most secret wish is to wake up as a gnome and spend his days building wooden locks, eating tiny biscuits and hanging out with birds. He can be found eating watermelon over the sink or online.

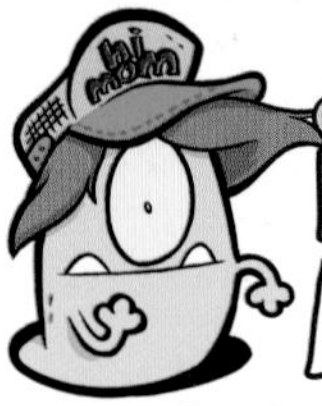
hi mom

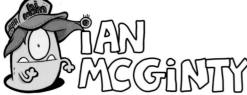

IAN MCGINTY

is a real smiley dude! And he wants to know where you got that cool lunchbox! You know, the one with the dinosaur riding a great white shark? Oh, is this Gilbert Johnson? No? Gosh, sorry for bothering you! Um...okay, bye.

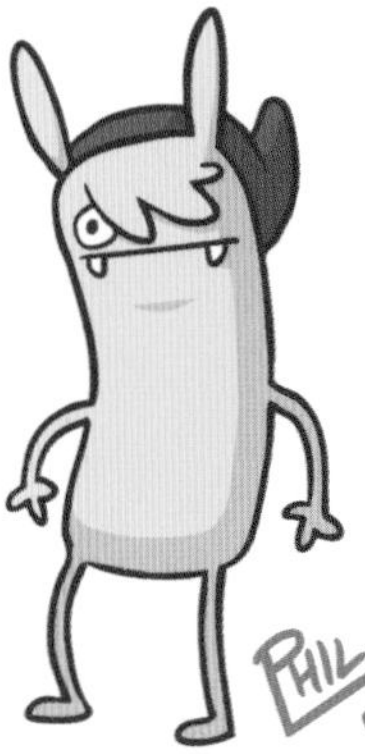
PHIL J.

PHILLIP JACOBSON

is a graduate of the Savannah College of Art and Design sequential art program. His earlier works include the self-published titles *Battle Mammals* and *Pancakes for Yeti*. Some of his influences include Bryan Lee O'Malley, Madeline Rupert and Craig Bartlett. He would like to thank his late grandmother Mary Ann Hill for constantly encouraging him to draw when he was little and for inspiring him to pursue his artistic goals.

TO YOU BY:

DEVILROBOTS

is a five-man design team. Established in 1997 and based in Tokyo, their main work consists of graphic design, character design, illustration, web design, project planning and production. Their work is known worldwide, especially in Asia.

DEVILROBOTS' sensibility is a little evil and robotic fun, and the result is an original world that is darkly cute. Their main character TO-FU OYAKO is well known worldwide.

THEO ELLSWORTH

can't stop drawing. He's always working on new comics, art zines, album art, and original wood cut characters and he never wants to stop! He very much enjoyed his visit to the world of Uglydolls and hopes to stop by again sometime. He lives in Montana with his witchdoctor wife and his son who loves trains. He rides his bike to his studio to draw every day. He's probably there right now.

MAD BARBARIANS

are an illustration/design unit from Japan comprised of Katsuya Saito and Masumi Ito with "Mad, Pop, Rock, Cute, and Stupid" as their main concept. They were founded in 2000 and are based in Japan. Because of the success of their original vinyl figures, they now participate in art shows and autograph sessions worldwide.

MAD BARBARIANS aim for world domination with MAD characters.

JUNKO MIZUNO

is a self-taught artist who is recognized for her unique style of powerful female imagery. In 1996, she self-produced a photocopy booklet called "MINA animal DX" which brought her to the attention of the publishing industry in Japan. Soon after, she debuted as a professional comic artist and illustrator. Currently residing in San Francisco, she is constantly working on new comics, paintings, illustrations and designs for products ranging from toys to clothing.

FRANK C. STRESING

is a comic book colorist on this book. Instilled with a love of cartoons at a young age, Fred started drawing and coloring in comics when he was three. He still does, only now he doesn't get yelled at for it.

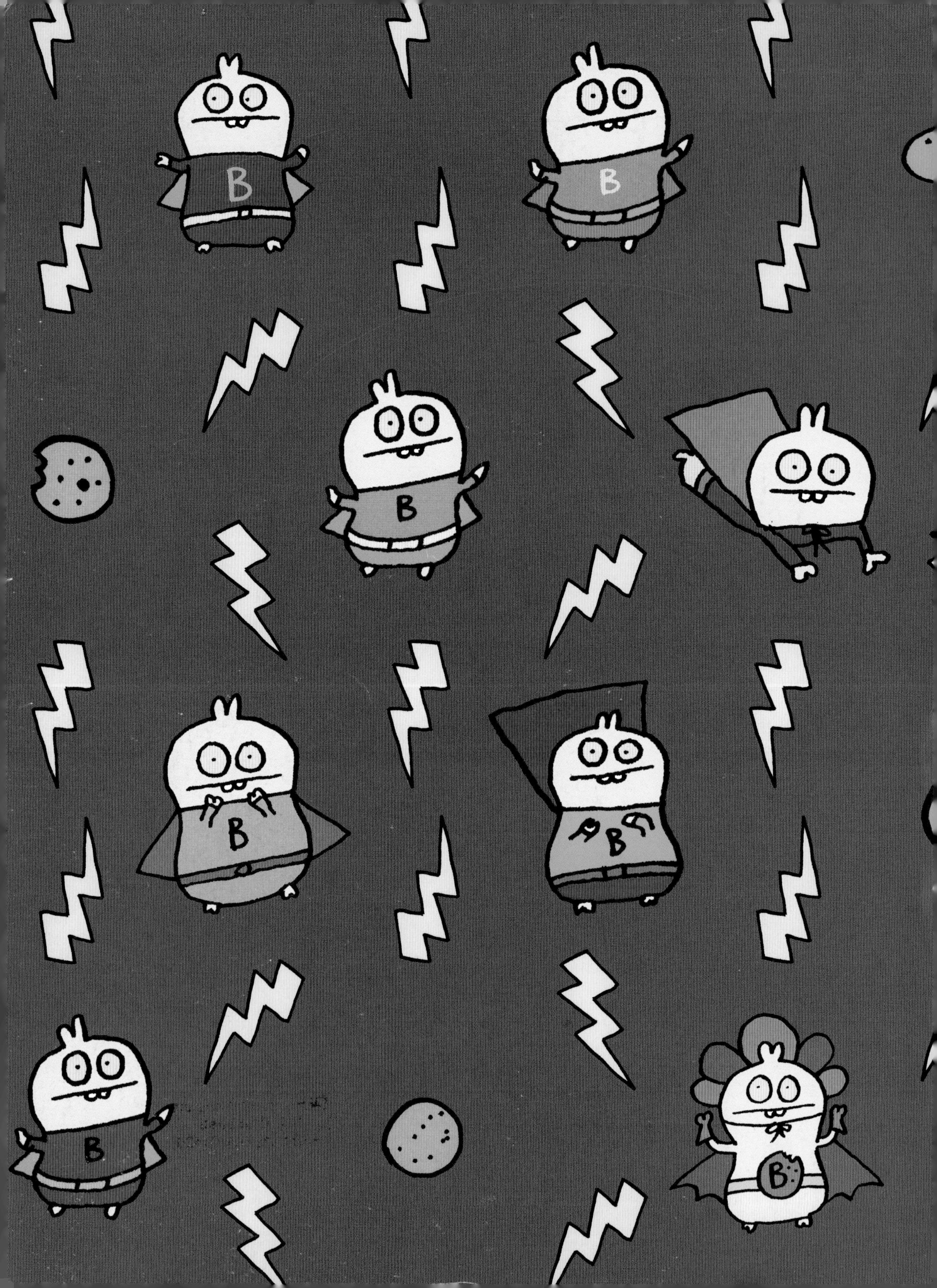